MUSCLE

MUSCLE

ALAN TROTTER

FABER & FABER

First published in 2019
by Faber & Faber Limited
Bloomsbury House
74–77 Great Russell Street
London WC1B 3DA

Typeset by Faber & Faber Limited
Printed and bound by CPI Group (UK) Ltd, Croydon, CR0 4YY

A CIP record for this book
is available from the British Library

ISBN 978–0–571–35221–0

10 9 8 7 6 5 4 3 2 1

For my parents

Prologue

The two men watch him cascade into the darkness, watch him tumble between the train tracks, his body spinning and broken, his arms snapping at him like whipping rope.

The smaller of the two, Hector he is called, lights a cigarette and says, 'So, what did we think of that?'

The other waits. His look is pointed as an asterisk. He waits and looks at his companion until he is handed the cigarette. He draws on it and, while Hector retrieves for himself a replacement, he speaks.

'Instinctively I suppose I enjoyed it,' he says. This second man is called Charles. 'It's obvious enough why. There is inherent drama in the transformation.'

'One moment he is a person,' says Hector, 'the next he is a clutch of broken pencils. He's blood and meat and roiling volition, and nothing else. And gone. Backwards and out of sight, leaving us to think about him.'

'Or we are gone,' Charles points out.

'Or we are gone. Of course you're right,' says Hector. 'We are on the train, which is moving ahead at speed, uninterrupted. It appeared as if he was pulled away from us, backwards, snatched into the night, only because we continued to travel forward at the full speed of the train.'

3

'There was a defiant, violent attempt at stillness—what else is a sudden exit from a moving train?—but momentum pulled at him as if he was bound to us at the waist. So he didn't bounce backwards as it appeared. In that first bounce he was moving forward, and at speed. He was moving forward faster, in that moment, than he had ever before moved, outside of being in a car, or on a horse if we imagine he had ever ridden one, or on a train.'

'One of the rush of new experiences that came to him all at the end.'

'All at the end, all at once. And then the second bounce and any that followed it in the dark—'

'There will have been some.'

'—were quickly slower, as his body resisted movement beyond its capacity to resist, breaking and turning, torn apart by the effort.'

Hector and Charles share in the loud silence of train travel, the exertions of the engine reduced by their regularity to a calming sidewise cradling.

The man had dropped something as they lifted him to the railing.

Hector kneels, inspecting the object where it trembles, insectile, from the movement of the train.

PART I

When _____ arrived in the city I was sitting outside a cafe. It was raining but not hard and I had been smoking a cig-arette and patting the ash onto the shoes of a sap at the table next to mine, a man whose moustache I had taken a disliking to. The sap left promptly, leaving me with no one to pat ash on and not much of a cigarette when _____ arrived.

_____ arrived thrown from a car. He led with his face, following with his knees, his arms back and up as if tied to his sides. When he hit the ground he somersaulted, and ended like a corpse on parade—flat on his back, legs and arms stiff-straight. The car that furnished him never com-pletely stopped, so all that remained of it, when his hat had done spinning like a coin in the dirt, was whatever of its exhaust still lingered. He was thrown more or less at my feet. Somehow _____ managed to look down his nose at me, as if I was lying in his gutter.

I offered him a cigarette and he took it, pulled himself up, cleared the grit from his hat and his face, and it came about that we got to talking.

I admired the way he could make an entrance like that and not take it too sore. He admired my height. Or any-way, he said he could use a man like me, and when people talk about me like that, as if I was a ladder or an adjustable wrench, it's usually my size they mean.

_____ spat a little blood and said that he could only stay in a city if it had a fairground and rollercoasters, and I said we had a fairground with three rollercoasters, so that's where we went.

We were told to remove our hats at the first rollercoaster, and we held them to our chests as it clack-clack-clacked us up high and then shook us all the way down again. I felt like a penny thrown down a drain or a man thrown from a moving car. _____ seemed to take it worse. When it was done he sat on a bench with his head between spread knees, a finger at each upper eyelid, compressing the sides of his eyeballs at a steady pace. He said it helped, he needed a reliable impression to attend to.

I asked him why we'd come to the fairground if he didn't like the rollercoasters, and he said he did like rollercoasters, and also that that was one of the better ones he'd been on.

Once he'd recovered we rode it again, and then tried the others. Our first time on the tallest of the three it happened that I sat in the front carriage, in front of _____. As we turned the tallest peak, the city seemed to tip out in front of me like dark paint down a glass hill. This view struck me like I just woke up, as if I'd never seen the city before, or else never really believed it real—three times the ride took us round and each time as we went over the peak, this same feeling charged me, as if I'd taken some of _____'s love for these rides from him. I was still sharp with the feeling as we got back on dull ground. Only then did I find that on account of my height, _____'s view had been impeded and his enjoyment impaired.

As we walked away from the rollercoaster, _____ with his drunkard's stagger, he didn't touch me or look at me, but he was speaking, and I realised he was talking to me, telling me that he would find me when I was asleep, he would stand over me and kick through my head, described the ear ripping off and the skull creasing then giving beneath his shoe. On the bench, as he pressed at his eyes, he finished snarling, then it was done, and we went back to riding the rollercoasters.

We rode each of the three rollercoasters in turn for the next four hours. Every half-hour or so _____ would need to sit on the bench and press his eyes, looking like a man who'd been poisoned, but as we made our way to the next ride he'd be lit with glee.

That night, as he had no money and no other place to go, _____ came home with me.

I got into bed next to him—an inverted _____, already snoring—and inches from my face were his naked toes, and I thought about his promise to drive this foot into my head. The hours at the fairground had left me slightly nauseous, I was in the tired, sense-drained final pull into sleep, and still charged by seeing the city tipped out below, and the threat too became part of a warm, muddled calm that was still there when I woke up.

The next day I made us breakfast and we went together to find _____ an apartment.

It was _____ that gave me the name Box. He never really explained it to me, and I never asked, not wanting to confront his generosity, but it spoke to me of an unassuming usefulness—and it stuck, and I was glad to have it.

It felt as if it had been weeks since I had found anything to do but sit by roads or in cafes. Or longer: for as far back as I could think, the best I could hope was that a fight or a conversation might break out nearby. Then _____ arrived and I had an expectation of relief.

Only there was none. Life continued to move forward with the brakes on tight.

Two things happened over a whole month with _____. The first was at a bus stop and meant nothing but struck me all the same.

I was to see _____ at his apartment and as the bus didn't arrive I grew angry. Angry at how long it would be until I was there, and also because I knew already that however long it took, I would still find _____ in his vest, and have to wait while he made himself coffee and washed his face.

Then a man limped to the stop: he had big jug ears that poured white hair, he had watery eyes and hands that shook. We stood together.

He said, 'The thing to do is light a cigarette,' and he

took a pack from his pocket. 'As soon as I light a cigarette, the bus arrives.' He lighted his cigarette and smoked it to the last breath, without any bus arriving, then somehow found a way to keep smoking it. Finally he put it out under his foot. I said something to him about his system being flawed. While I spoke he looked at my mouth like I was a stumbling idiot and only the thought that maybe he was limited in his hearing stopped me from laying him flat. When I'd got it out he said, 'Ah, the thing is you can't always tell which cigarette it's going to be,' and he lighted another, and from around the corner turned our bus.

On the bus ride, I spent my time looking at my packet of cigarettes, wondering if somehow I'd smoked the wrong pill on the wrong street corner and I had brought _____ tumbling to my feet. Maybe I would do well to be more cautious about lighting cigarettes, or else I'd light one and another car would tear its way through the street, and out from the door, his arms back and up, would come another _____. It wouldn't need to happen often, just maybe every hundred or two hundred or three cigarettes, and another _____ would come out until they lined the gutter, until they started to pile up like cards in a deck.

The other thing that happened during that month was nearly a job until it wasn't.

_____ tried to find us work but he had no plan for going about it. We would set out from _____'s apartment, pursue a circuit, and as we went we'd see a key-cutter or a florist and _____ would make an approach. This didn't come easily to him. Violence was all we had to offer, and there must have been those who wanted it, but it was too obvious in _____'s pitch, too close. Instead we got no work, and left a trail behind us of confused and intimidated key-cutters and florists and road sweepers, which we'd add to until one or other of us grew tired of the parade. At which point we'd take ourselves to a bar, where _____ would drink beer while I dwelt on what exactly I'd expected from him, and from us.

We repeated this like a circuit on a ghost train where every ghost was an intimidated sweep, key-cutter, spot-welder or meter reader, and repeated it for days, until we hit on what seemed to be some good luck.

First thing that morning we passed a woman on the street, who was not much older than twenty and standing alongside a van maybe twice her age. She was turning a handle that fit into the vehicle's chest—the whole side of it was open to copper ribs, a device for the production of coffee, and the handle, we found out, was fixed to a grinder.

We bought coffee from her and it was dark and thick in tall mugs. As we drank it, _____ asked the woman if she had any work that needed doing, and maybe because _____ was occupied with his coffee and this altered the impression he made, she didn't recoil from him, but asked what kind of thing he meant. _____ suggested maybe she was owed some money, or there could be someone who had taken advantage of her one way or another, or perhaps an ex-lover. She said she'd think it over. We drank the hot, heavy coffee.

She said the longer she thought about it the more she realised she knew some kind, decent people, and she should be grateful for that. Because honestly if you asked her would she like to see any of these people have their teeth punched out of them or be made earnestly to fear for their life, then the answer was no. We finished our coffee, gave her back the cups and she reached into the guts of the van to rinse them.

We went on with a feeling, maybe from the coffee, which was good, together with the outlook of the woman, which seemed good too, that we should stick to our circuit and we'd be rewarded. And before two hours had passed we were in the back room of a clockmaker's, and he was telling us that there was a customer who owed him money and maybe we could get it back for him.

The clockmaker was fat—as round as a watch face. He kept the back room of his shop cold, every window open, but still he kept wiping the sweat from his brow. He had been a military man once, he told us, and it had hit his head like a hammer hits an alarm bell, so now he had neuroses, and there were people who took advantage of them. For one thing, he could no longer be in the same room as anything that resembled a military uniform, whether it was a uniform on a policeman or a cigarette girl. Even as he spoke sweat sprang from every degree round the big circle of his face. Weapons too, he said: if a shadow reminded him too much of a barrel of a gun it could freeze him in his chair until some change of the light saved him. And he told us all this, because there was a time when he would have taken care of this customer himself, but now he was constitutionally unable. But then we had arrived to him. Like grace, he said, like daybreak.

For the first time we had work. The clockmaker gave this man to us, a customer who had taken advantage of his weakness: he gave us the name, and the name of the joint the man owned and worked as a counterman. He said that we should go to him, take what money we could and retrieve a wristwatch that the man would be wearing.

_____ had started twitching in his seat with anticipation, like he was grease in a hot pan. He started talking. He suggested that we might bust the customer's nose. He said we might cut him up. A storm reached the clockmaker's face, his big cheeks fluttered like tent canvas in the wind, but _____ didn't see it: he swung his butterfly knife out from his pocket and its handle, and held it to his own throat as part of his play about what we'd do to the customer. The clockmaker's face parted so wide and quick it might have been split with an axe, and as he shrieked he came over the top of his table and drove us out before him with his great chest, until we were back in the street and the door of the shop slammed tight.

From having our first piece of work to having nothing and being back on the street went so quick that we stood for a moment while the situation asserted itself.

_____ laughed and said he would come back later, when the clockmaker had calmed down, and he would speak to him again and the job would be back on, and he slapped me friendly on the cheek.

Later though I watched through the door as one of _____'s hand slipped across the large, wet face of the clockmaker and the other drove short punches with the small knife through straining waistcoat fabric, which striped with blood.

Outside I asked him how the talk had gone. The job was back on, he said.

So we went to the joint the clockmaker had given us, to find the man who owed him money. We sat, and spent the day smoking cigarettes, drinking coffee, drinking water. _____ would pour liquor into his coffee from a flask. The clockmaker's customer worked the counter. He pinkened every time I caught his eye.

As the place emptied he started sending us free coffee, free food. We ignored it. He had the expensive wristwatch on. This man pleading poverty: a romantic, clinging to heirlooms. Eventually, darkness filled the room like cold coffee, and the waitress lit the dim fluorescent night.

At closing the counterman had her ask us to leave. I kept my eyes on him, while she tried her best, but timidly. _____ put out one finger, and used it to tip a cup onto its side. The cup rang a small sharp note as it hit the table top, and the waitress ran away like she was chased.

The counterman straightened his apron and organised his courage in a little heap and stepped out from behind his bench. Before he was halfway to our table we stood and left. We heard him, relief flooding out as anger, yelling at the waitress, and she got the door locked tight behind us.

And then we met him that night as he took the garbage out the back.

We got better at finding work after that, but it still didn't come easy. _____ had to bully work out of people. He had to have me shake work out of them. We were given some people to scare, a few hands to break.

After some months, word started to get around that we were the people to go to if you needed a hand broken. In this city, that was a lot of hands. You'd be surprised. It was all we ever seemed to do: find people, young men mostly, and then break hands. Dried blood began to clog the metallic lighter I'd place between their middle and ring fingers.

We grew bored.

_____ wanted to approach Jarecki, but Jarecki was a notoriously difficult figure to approach.

Jarecki owned half the city, Danskin the other half. Their nearness in size made the peace between them a particular kind of uneasy. The difference between them couldn't have been much more than the weight of a single bill, but each eyed the scale and felt sure it fell in his own favour.

The lesser man in any setup is always prone to indignities—raids, passing money up, receiving judgement when he gets above his station. Every so often, in all kinds of ways, he's made to pay. Both Jarecki and Danskin thought the other should be suffering, so both made it happen. There were incursions, there was payback: the friction was constant, but didn't often throw up so many sparks as to impede business.

But it was a difficult atmosphere for a paranoid man, and Jarecki was a very paranoid man. Regularly, we knew, he would disappear from sight, convinced that Danskin was plotting to assassinate him, or that the police were preparing a raid, and in the meantime his proxies were left to manage his operation.

This was during a long absence for Jarecki, but we visited his club anyway. It was one of the two big gambling joints in the city (the other was Danskin's).

_____ went to curse at waitresses and dealers, demanding to see Jarecki. They looked at him with the blankness of good discipline. He might as well have tried to shake some better news out of the man on the television set.

I watched two gamblers playing blackjack. A child or a dog can learn basic blackjack strategy by rote in twenty minutes. Stick with a hard total of nineteen. Double down on eleven if the dealer's got anything but an ace showing. Nothing in blackjack exists on a more complicated level than this. The gamblers were solemn with their cards and their chips. They weighed their options and tugged on their cuffs and tossed back their whiskies and then did exactly what they were always going to do. They didn't seem sharp to the fact that the house was winning not because of some flaw in their tactics, but because the house is meant to win.

You sit down to a game of blackjack and you begin to exist at two speeds at once. The excitement comes from the leaps you make from one hand to the next—up or down a bill (or twenty, or a hundred, or whatever it is you need to get excited). A good hand and your winnings jump up a step; a few good hands in a row and you really feel like you're climbing somewhere. But you're making all your leaps inside a train car which is being borne slowly, steadily downhill. Because the house has the edge.

In everything there's a house edge. The house edge is the average amount you lose relative to any bet you make. On straights in roulette, the house edge is the five and twenty you lose every hundred. When you get arrested in the city it's the one time in three the police choose to fix you a beating. The individual leap is what you concentrate on when you sit down to a hand of blackjack, and the hands are skittish individuals, but the house edge is the larger container, and it moves at a slower, truer speed. The house edge is reliable as death.

The two gamblers had dreamed away the house edge. It made them boring.

Meanwhile _____'s strategy collapsed quickly. Every dealer on the floor had made the same argument to him in their own way: no they didn't know a Jarecki, no _____ couldn't see him, and either he was going to gamble or he was going to leave. Then two more men appeared from behind a curtain to make the point again. The smaller had the look animals get when they've grown accustomed to being beaten by the people they rely on for food and care. The larger had a nose that had been broken so many times it lay flat on his face like roadkill.

Roadkill laid his hand on _____'s shoulder. _____ shook it off and attempted to tip over a roulette table, to shrieks from the opera crowd, who fled across the room, putting some space and their women between _____ and their chips.

From the back room behind the curtain came a third man. He had grey fuzz for hair, sharp features and a cold eye for _____. This was a man called Fylan, one of Jarecki's proxies. _____ dodged to Fylan and started to introduce himself. Roadkill caught up to him and laid a firmer hand this time. I left for the cloakroom.

By the time I was outside, _____ had already been deposited there. I gave him his hat and helped him off the ground. I said his strategy had collapsed quickly. He showed me a wallet and a watch and explained that the wallet belonged to the big man with the mistreated nose, and the watch belonged to Fylan, the proxy.

Neither had been missed yet, he said, but someone would come to recover them. He was going to continue to irritate them until he got what he wanted.

I dragged a mattress up the stairs to _____'s apartment and we set to waiting.

*

The apartment manager was fond of _____. He'd bring up ice in a bucket and talk to _____ while I'd sit with the bucket between my feet and work at it with an ice pick. They'd have glasses of scotch on the rocks and I'd have a tall glass of ice chips (I didn't care much for drink, which tended to make me feel too much like my head might tip off my shoulders if I made a sudden move). I'd suck on ice chips and listen to them talk.

They talked about horses, which the apartment manager liked to play. He'd explain that he had just figured out why he'd never been a winner and now that he knew he was going to start winning big. Then he'd wait for _____ to ask him about it. He liked _____ even though _____ never did ask about his system.

The apartment manager would say that in all his years of cursed luck he'd never managed to lose his wife in a bet however hard he tried, and then he'd laugh until he left to get more. He'd talk about the cars and apartments and women he'd buy when he started winning and he talked about what he'd do with me if he could afford to have us do favours for him. A big guy like me, he figured, could do things to a lot of guys he knew deserved it.

His wife's brother could take some hurting, could lose an inch or two in height and a pint or so of blood, he reckoned. There was a policeman who'd insisted on hauling him to court to answer a phoney vagrancy charge when all he'd done was have some drinks and forget how much coppers liked to be curtsied to and doted on. There was a woman in the building who'd no money because of all the hop she was taking—when the time came to pay the rent they'd reached an arrangement and he'd gotten something that still burned where you don't tell the ladies. When he'd had a job at the racetrack, helping out in the stables, one time a horse came in that was more handsome than any animal he'd ever seen, so he'd put some money on it, and it won. He loved hamburger, the apartment manager, thought it was the finest food there was, and don't try and tell him otherwise. So he figured the horse would like hamburger too and figured to treat it for the win. But the horse choked on the meat. He lost the job at the track and the son of a bitch who owned the horse shouted into his face for a good hour and more. He was sure I could do wonderful things with a thonged blackjack and that dumb horse owner's teeth.

He gave _____ thin black cigarettes from a metal case and lighted them for him. I sucked my ice chips and listened. We watched the rain for four days, and it never once stopped.

_____ wanted me around all the time, but in the mornings when I'd watch him climb out of his bed and his shins walk past my mattress, he'd unlock the door of the apartment and I'd go for a walk, take the chance to stretch my legs.

One of those nights, while we were waiting, the apartment manager's wife came up as well. She had a drink and talked about how unhappy her marriage was. Occasionally the apartment manager would help her out, reminding her of the start of a story about just how unhappy they were together, then pass her a black cigarette. She told good stories, and a dirty joke as well as anyone you ever knew.

My back had been hurting from leaning down to chip ice, so I had taken to sitting on the ground with the bucket between my thighs. A while into one of her jokes she patted the skirt that sat up over her knees and I moved over and sat between her calves. She told the rest of her joke and stroked her hands through my hair and when she finished and I was roaring with laughter she patted my head and rubbed at my shoulders roughly, appreciatively, and I moved further into the vein-outlined world of those legs. The apartment manager blew smoke rings from his black cigarettes and scratched at the itch the hop smoker had given him.

On the fourth day I came back to the apartment from stretching my legs and found that our waiting was done. The broken nose and his smaller, beaten friend were there. Roadkill was clearly already sore to find that _____ didn't contain apologies, and it only soured his mood when I appeared.

Maybe he thought me coming up the stairs was a deliberate move—the two of us boxing them in. Anyway he lowered his head and charged me back into the railing of the stairs, but I got a low uppercut in before he reached me and I felt the nose give, though it didn't stop him coming.

He had me pushed into the railing and my arms pinned, but he was clumsy and I kicked his legs out from under him. His head caught the side of the railing as he went down. He made a move to get back on his feet that was more bullheaded than graceful, so I used a fist to make sure he'd stay put.

_____ already had his smaller friend on the ground and was beating him with a belt. I took a moment to catch my breath and see if any of my ribs were broken. When _____'s arm got tired he went to his desk and wrote something out, then pulled off the sheet of paper and came over to me.

There was blood around his mouth but I couldn't see where he'd been biting the smaller man. He often bit. Once, among our hand-breaking, I had seen him bite through a man's cheek and pull out one of his teeth with his own. The only explanation he'd given was to say that it was already loose.

_____ stuffed the piece of paper half in Roadkill's fly, pressed the lifted wallet into his jacket, and together we dragged the pair of them to the stairs and sent them sliding down the first flight.

The next visit we had was a telegram. It took us back to Jarecki's casino the next evening.

The re-ruined nose met us in the club. It had been built into a thick package of gauze—two small plastic straws sticking out where the nostrils would be. It led us through to a hidden door set into the back wall. When the door cracked I could see Fylan standing in front of a large carved desk.

_____ told me to wait outside. I didn't want to mess things up without cause, so I stood and killed time listening to the breath whistling through those straws.

After a while, Roadkill spoke, told me his name was Bernard.

He told me I'd picked a bad one to arm for.

I told him that wasn't how _____ and I worked.

'Right,' he said. 'I speak to a lot of brains out here in the cold.'

After that we didn't talk much.

When _____ came out we had our first favour from Jarecki. _____ waved a piece of paper at me. He said there was a name and an address, and we were to search the place. I asked _____ what it was we were meant to find, and he explained that we were just meant to search.

The soft, pale man lived on the outskirts of everything. As soon as he saw us at his door he began apologising. It was as if he had just delivered us some bad news, and he felt cut up about it, eager to make reparations. As we went in, _____ reassured him that he had nothing to apologise for, which as far as we know could be true, though the odds are always against it.

_____ started feeling along the seam of the cushions on his seats, then slicing them open and poking around inside with his knife, like he expected to wake something sleeping in there. I unrolled the blind, standing clear to let anything that might drop out drop. And when it didn't I peered up behind it and then, to get a better view of the nothing that was up there, tugged it down.

_____ called him Truford and asked him where it was. Truford looked at his toes like they were embarrassing him. _____ knocked down a couple of vases and asked again where it was. Truford claimed not to know what it was we wanted, which, if it was true, made all of us.

_____ swept his arm through a shelf of plates and then used his shoe to rake through the pieces. It could be anywhere, anywhere at all.

I threw everything out from the cupboard underneath the sink and a bottle—bleach, by the smell—started leaking on the floor.

It might be tucked or taped behind a pipe, so I felt around behind the pipes. It was obvious before I touched one of them that I was going to burn myself on it, I could feel the heat off it, but it had to be checked. Still the burn annoyed me, and I tugged on one of the other pipes, just enough that a thin spray of water began pissing itself up against the underside of the sink.

_____ kicked loose some baseboard, then pried it free with his hands. In the bathroom I emptied the pills from their containers and the containers out of the mirrored cabinet, and pulled the cabinet off the wall. I cut the toothpaste tube open and pulled down the curtain rail from the shower and peered along its hollow, empty length. In the bedroom I pulled the pockets and the lining off the only jacket he seemed to own and filleted his mattress and pillow.

Truford was sitting on the guts and springs of one of his chairs, like a fat angel on a broken cloud. _____ asked him again where it was. He still doesn't know, he said, which is or isn't the same as he doesn't know what it is. _____ separated the two pictures hanging on the wall from their frames. Neither showed Truford. I guess there's no space for a man like Truford even on his own walls.

The search must have gone well, because it wasn't long before Bernard came to the door with another job. His nose was still bandaged, but only over the bridge, so he didn't need the straws to breath any more. This time he came with a Mexican boy of about fifteen. He spoke to _____ while the boy did nothing but flip a knife open and shut, open and shut.

I'm too large to make much of a tail and I sneak a bit better than I ice skate, but the work for Jarecki didn't tend to the subtle, and made the time pass.

Say the well-loved daughter of a well-connected father fell for a tough, and the tough's paws turned fist too easy. The father would go to Jarecki, we would go visit the tough. The friends of a new dealer at the club come to visit him at his table and the house obligingly loses to them—

we would go and see how their luck stood up to a test. We'd be given somebody; we'd extract apologies, reparations, we'd ease the flow of regret.

We also turned down a few favours from Jarecki. As when _____ didn't want to scare a girl back to work after she'd run off with a john. He'd realised that the madam, more romantic than most and caring for the girl, was, in this instance, for love conquering all. So when we let it, the madam grew a soft spot for _____, which suited him down to the ground. Other favours he turned down for less identifiable reasons. And we did favours on the side for people other than Jarecki, so we stayed what you'd call independents.

As far as I could call it, _____ only ever spoke to Fylan, the proxy, and never to Jarecki himself.

When there wasn't work we threw cards into a hat, or we listened to the apartment manager's stories while I chipped ice, or we rode the rollercoasters. I didn't want to drag my mattress anywhere else, so I kept sleeping at the foot of _____'s bed.

I woke into darkness and to the sound of _____'s bed springs.

_____ had a routine when he would wake. First he would sit up, then he would cough for a while, a prolonged fit of coughing, like he was a cage that he had to rattle to make sure he was all awake, down inside as well and not just got his eyes open. I listened to him go through this cough—which sounds like it hurts but gives him satisfaction—then spit into the handkerchief he keeps by his bed for the purpose. Then he stood and I expected him to step over me on his way to piss and dress, and instead I got a kick in the ribs, hard as I ever have.

I'd thought before about whether _____ would ever try to kill me: how he would go about it. The threats, beginning with the first day at the fairground, didn't worry me. I had learned that this was the sort of thing he threatened everyone with, and rarely did he mean it. But it was also true that we'd done things together in the course of our favours for Jarecki, and there are things you do with a person, shared experiences, that you'd be stupid not to hold in your mind when considering their character. These recollections aren't something you could easily rid yourself of. It would be like digging a tick from your skin—the mouth can tear off and stay behind, still biting.

When I took the kick to my ribs I was on my side, and I tried to jack-knife my legs up to knock _____ to the ground before he did whatever he was going to do next. But instead the pain made me buckle, set me clutching at my chest, and I thought I was going to vomit. It must have looked pretty funny.

I was expecting, I guess, _____'s knife across my face or into my belly, or for him to stamp on me. Instead he mumbled something and shambled away and the lights in the bathroom flicked on, and I could hear him pissing.

When he came back out I was still clutching at my ribs,

and he patted me on the shoulder and then took the glass of water that I keep by the leg of his bed, filled it up and brought it back to me. Which was white of him, and not something he'd do if he hadn't regretted the mistake. Then he went through to the main room.

After a while he was joined by some noise at the door and then a couple of voices.

When it was clear at least one of my ribs had broken and the pain was going to make sleep impossible, I followed.

_____ was dealing cards to the apartment manager—who was talking about some leg show he'd seen—and to a space at the table where a black cigarette burned in an ashtray. Once he'd dealt they did a round of betting, folding the empty seat when its turn arrived. _____ was dealing the flop when the apartment manager's wife came back in the room.

I pulled a chair up beside her and watched as they played, the apartment manager's wife showing me her hands. Lydia she's called—why shouldn't she deserve a name?

Showing cards like that is a compliment. It shows you trust the other person not to give any hint of what the hand is like, and it's intimate. You get a better idea of how someone else plays the game when they're showing you their hands than you will any other way. You don't let someone see your weaknesses like that. Women do, I guess, when they like you. And it's okay, when it's like it was with Lydia.

When she folded a hand pre-flop she'd tell one of her jokes, and we'd all laugh, though laughing hurt my ribs. Sometimes when she got to the end of a joke, her eyes would lock with the apartment manager's and they'd say the last line of the joke loudly and in time, like it was a line from a song, and already laughing, and then you'd kind of see why they'd ended up together.

Eventually I left the three playing and slept with the pain. Though whenever I wasn't lying flat on my back any more I woke up to hear about it.

The poker games began to happen weekly, sometimes twice a week. Normally just with _____, the apartment manager and Lydia. Sometimes with one or two friends of the apartment manager, people he knew from the track, who bet big, hurriedly, eager to lose and recreate the thrill of losing on the horses.

When someone took a break I'd sit in for them, or else Lydia would show me her hands, or else I'd just sleep and never mind the game in the main room.

When _____ plays poker with people he hasn't played with before, he begins by playing cautiously. If he starts off betting big, no one believes him. People think they know a man like _____ very quickly. If they met him twice they'd think they knew all there was to know. And they guess from the type of man they think he is that he's going to play recklessly.

He could win by betting like that, I'd seen him do it a

couple of times, but only because the people he's playing with are too scared to beat him. When they fold to a raise it's not because they think he's got them outmatched, it's because they think it would embarrass _____ if they called him and he had to admit a dud hand, and they think the chips are not worth whatever _____ might do to someone who embarrassed him.

So instead _____ begins slowly, he plays even good hands gently, until they come to believe he's a man who can control his temper, who won't go all in on a jack high and a sore head, but can wait for the cards and then play them the way they deserve.

_____ plays cards like a saint.

I sat outside and shared some silence with Bernard while _____ was in talking to Fylan. By now Bernard's nose was only ribbed with thin, slightly bloodied strips of bandage, a raised ripe scab down its crooked middle. At one point he looked almost like he was going to offer me a cigarette, which was white of him.

_____ came out with our instructions and we walked four blocks to a hotel called the Elmwood, though only an 'm' still clung to the wall outside, the other letters readable in the embarrassed, clean spaces they had left behind.

We got past the desk and up to our floor without difficulty. _____ took his butterfly knife from his pocket. He flicked his hand and the blade opened out and then was clinched again at the base by the two sides of the handle.

Before he moved toward the door I asked if maybe he minded if I had a go picking this one. _____ pursed his lips for a moment, not like he was really considering, and then explained that he was better at this than me, which was true, and what if I botched it and then the guy comes in, not an unsuspecting sap but alert and on edge, with every chance to get a rod out?

I thought about how was I ever going to get any better at it without a chance to practise? But this was a conversation we'd had before and I was not in a mood to go through it again. It would end, I knew, with mention of one occasion when my frustration led to a door being kicked from its frame.

So _____ got the door open and we went in.

The hotel needed better maid service or better guests. Clothes caked the two chairs, the desk and the floor, a towel was drying on the bedsheets and an ashtray overflowed onto the pillow at the head of the bed.

_____ looked around and then removed his homburg and tucked himself in behind the curtain with a gesture to follow. The curtain was already drawn over the window. You could see his shape extruding from it—a man in outline, hat held to his chest, and below the curtain, a pair of shoes. But two pairs of shoes under a curtain is no more conspicuous than one, so I crept in alongside him.

We stood and we waited. Maybe _____ could make some claim to being hidden—only because I was acting as a tent pole, sheltering him: I was a big dumb ghost in a sheet, with a smaller ghost hiding in his skirts. It got dark.

Our sap came in and flipped on the light. We waited for him to spy the newly risen mounds in his curtain. With the light on we could see him through the material, and he was singing a show tune to himself. He had to see us. We couldn't have been more visible if we'd been nude. If we'd been alight. If we'd had stage names and faces from the paper and spotlights trained on us.

But he tossed his jacket on a chair, spun a merry spin on the balls of his feet, and finished his song with his hands on his hips, his back to the window and his head in easy reach of _____'s blackjack.

So _____ reached.

We snapped bracelets on the unconscious sap, slung him in a chair and waited some more.

_____ smoked a cigarette. The sap hadn't paid enough to get a toilet of his own so I pissed in the sink, in a swirling, difficult manner. It all risked the kind of mistake that would have been taken out on the sap's cheap hide, but I stayed dry and he got lucky.

The phone rang and _____ glanced at his wristwatch and ignored it. We let it ring for as long as it cared to. In the chair, the sap slept soundly on.

We kicked our heels until the phone rang again. _____ checked the time and picked up the receiver, and spoke without waiting, telling them to send him up. I took a guess that 'him' would be Fylan.

_____ considerately took the ring off his right hand and slapped the sap's face back and forth a couple of times, and I took the opportunity to get rid of the rest of a glass of water by throwing it over him. The sap's head lolled side to side and his mouth began chewing on vowels and letting them drip off him with the water.

The sap's eyes were just agreeing to work together in the pursuit of common goals when they located Fylan, and an amount of fear shot through them that it's not an easy thing to earn. I felt impressed with Fylan, his ability to incite this wide-eyed animal terror in the hand-cuffed man. I already knew I liked him. The impression he always gave—in the way he moved and the way he talked—was one of nothing being wasted, not a movement, or a thought, or a mercy.

He asked us to leave the room. I'd reached the door and had it open when I realised that _____ wasn't behind me. He was peering over Fylan's shoulder at the sap. It took Fylan turning around and looking him in the eye and asking again before _____ understood that it wasn't just big lugs like me that had to wait outside.

In the corridor, _____ and I talked about how we'd hidden behind the curtain with the blackjack. We discussed how unlikely it was that even a dumb sap like the one we clearly had on our hands would miss us. Would miss us and then wander directly over to the curtain, and then obligingly turn, as if presenting his hatless crown for the blackjack. We had started to talk percentages and odds when Fylan opened the door and called us in.

He said there were a couple of things he had to check out, and depending on how well informed the man in the chair turned out to be, he might have a few follow-up questions to present to him.

And then Fylan breezed.

I sat on the edge of the bed and watched as _____ tipped back the brim of his homburg and started to light a cigarette. But just as he had his hand cupped around the flame, he stopped, shook out his match and put the pill away again. He said we should have a bet, put a fin on it.

He went over and snapped his fingers in front of the eyes of the sap in the chair. 'Buddy,' he said, looking to see if he was awake. The sap was awake, but struggling at it. _____ clicked his fingers a couple more times. When the sap had begun to pay attention to him, _____ lay his blackjack across his head, knocking him cold.

Then _____ knelt down in front of the again-unconscious sap, unlocked and removed his handcuffs. He picked up my hat from where I'd left it, shoved it at my chest and told me to come on, then we hid behind the curtain again.

We must have waited back there a half-hour, our bodies shaping the curtain like we were lying under a cover, our toes chilling themselves in the room, before a groaning came from the chair. The sap rubbed his head where he'd been twice laid out by the blackjack. He kept groaning and was saying some pretty restrained things about the Almighty, considering, when he seemed to realise that rubbing his head like he was meant he wasn't in bracelets any more, and all at once he leapt from the seat. _____ jabbed at me with his elbow, edging over so he could see better through the split. The sap looked around the room. Then he opened the outside door and looked both ways along the corridor. Not so much as a curious glance at the shapes in his curtains. Then, filled with resolve he ran over to his jacket, grabbed it from its chair, threw it on, seized his hat, and stood in front of us with his hands on his hips looking around for anything else he might have needed. _____ reached forward with the blackjack.

We came out and stood over the sap, looking down on him like a mouse who'd been given a maze to run and was curled up at the start gnawing its own leg.

I handed _____ a fin, and we dragged him back to his chair, put him back in the cuffs and waited for Fylan to return or for the phone to ring.

One night they were joined in their card game by a scrawny kid, making four of them: _____, the apartment manager, Lydia, showing me her hands, and this kid.

The kid was talking plenty to begin with. He was not saying much, but he was talking. He was the sort that holds a cigarette only in ways that don't quite make sense, like they've over-thought the whole exercise and now worry it won't be impressive enough just to hold a cigarette.

It was a friendly game and accordingly the chips were pretty sociable, passing the time with everybody in turn—but when this kid won a stack, pride would colour his face and his back would straighten right out. It was his dignity standing to attention. It was like seeing a corpse jump to its feet and give itself a round of applause.

Whenever this happened, Lydia would tell a joke, distracting from the display, because she's a good one and because it was embarrassing, watching the kid win. If you give yourself a parade every time you take a hand, it's a cinch you're not the kind of person it's hard to read. Win like that, no one with any sense has to watch it happen too often.

And then the kid started getting bad hands and kept playing them. It was clear they were bad because he gummed up. He was still okay in chips, but he wasn't even laughing at Lydia's jokes, and she tells a dirty joke as well as anyone you ever knew. But he kept raising, and losing, and when he lost his back crimped up.

You could have beaten him at cards dead drunk in a dark room so long as you had a protractor to take the angle of his spine.

The kid became a regular. He also had a name—Holcomb. He played cards and he drank and he never seemed to get any better at either. And he talked, which he could do.

Sometimes he talked like he was sitting at his own death-bed, reminiscing with himself. Sometimes he talked about girls he'd bought, and directed the worst of it at Lydia, as if he thought he could drive her to a fainting couch. Sometimes he talked like he was the first man to discover unhappiness and was deeply proud of the achievement.

There was one hand late in an evening where Holcomb was almost out of his chair with excitement right from the deal, but the apartment manager was too drunk to notice. No one else wanted anything to do with the hand. Lydia had one arm across her belly, the other pressing a black cigarette to her lips, the lips much more red than normal. She was in a mean mood: sometimes the day after a mood like this and with her husband on a drunk, you'd see him wondering what he'd done to get almost markless but painful wounds on his arms, and on one occasion a ciga-rette burn in the centre of his back up between his shoul-der blades, right where he couldn't reach it or quite see it properly, that had him running out his door whenever he heard feet on the steps to get someone else to take a look and give him word on what exactly was back there.

So Lydia began laughing at the apartment manager as he kept raising. The kid Holcomb is helium at this point. And of course it ended as a big win for Holcomb. Though it's less a win for the player than it is for the cards, in this instance. He raked the chips to himself and then lighted a new cigarette, and as the next hand was being dealt he gave a wave over his part of the table like a magician over a coin trick that meant he wanted dealt out.

While the other three played the hand, and for the next couple of hands as well, he started to talk about the story of Red Riding Hood, which I'd heard, and the Grimm brothers, who he seemed to think were quite the deal but were news to the rest of us. And he said that in the story of Red Riding Hood a little girl has been sent through the woods to visit her sick grandmother. And a bad wolf knows this, because he speaks to Red Riding Hood, and for some reason she gives him the straight tip on it. And the wolf goes ahead to grandma's house and eats the old lady and dresses in her old lady nightclothes and climbs into her bed and waits for Red Riding Hood.

Lydia showed me the low pair in her hand and then folded it to a modest raise from _____. She picked up her cigarette and said that she didn't know about the rest of the table but she'd had a childhood and parents and—(she drew a circle with the smoke to say, and so on). She seems older when she's in a mean mood. She tells fewer jokes, though they're just as funny. I was thinking I might take a glass of milk and go get some sleep.

Holcomb took a long draw on his pill and piped the smoke from the corner of his mouth, first in a thin stream, then, as the smoke kept on, in little rhythmic darts that still kept coming until it seemed the breath must have been spent, and then there was another squirt of smoke, and all the time his eyes fixed on Lydia. Finally he was done, and he continued his story.

According to the Grimm brothers, Red Riding Hood arrives and admires the wolf's eyes and ears and teeth, and the wolf eats her up, and then a hunter comes by. And the hunter cuts open the wolf with a scissors and gets Red Riding Hood and the grandma out, and piles rocks into the wolf in their place, and then sews the wolf up again. And it's having a belly full of rocks that does for the wolf in the end.

But, Holcomb says, the wolf's still lucky. Even the wolf in the next story, that no one remembers, the wolf that ends drowned in grandma's gutter chasing the sausage smell of cooking water is lucky. Because a twist like Red Riding Hood is always going to find a story to be a part of— some characters just have adventures thrown at them— but what's so special about a big, dumb animal with big teeth and big claws and no sense? And the grandma—if she didn't have Red Riding Hood as an affectionate, selfless granddaughter, what are the chances she'd get to be in any stories? She'd just be an old woman, sick and bed-bound, alone in the woods.

So, another version of the story, Holcomb says: Red Riding Hood's on her way to grandma's, and the wolf talks to her and then goes on ahead and devours grandma, but Red Riding Hood is distracted by another adventure, another story going on in the other direction through the woods, with a witch, or brothers turned into swans, or some bears instead of a big cruel wolf. So the wolf waits in bed, in grandma's nightclothes, with the grandma's sheets pulled up to its neck, but Red Riding Hood doesn't come, and the wolf keeps waiting.

'And after waiting for so long in the too-small bed,' he goes on, 'the wolf's back begins to hurt, so as he scours the shelves of the house for something to eat, he finds that he's begun to walk with a stoop. And as winter draws in, his feet are always sore and he has to rub them before trying to stand. And the wolf's big eyes are no longer as good for seeing anything with, and the wolf's ears can barely hear the wind whipping at the walls of the cottage, and the wolf's teeth hurt whenever he bites anything, and he's glad when one would fall out. And soon the wolf has no appetite at all and the nightclothes that used to bind his legs they were so tight, well, they hang loosely on him. And the wolf comes to think of himself as living in another wood, a wood within the cottage within the wood, an interior wood where each tree is another ache somewhere in his old body, and all the trees grow unnoticeably bigger day by day by day. And still his granddaughter hasn't come to bring him some cake or a bottle of wine. And his hair is matted and thinned, and sometimes in the morning he finds clumps of it in his bed, which he carefully tidies, because it's important to keep the place, even if no one is coming. And still the forest of aches in the wolf grows bigger and its branches more elaborately entwine, and he forgets ever living anywhere but amongst its dull pains and occasional sharp agonies in his small cottage, as his memory fades and dims.'

And he blew smoke from his cigarette, a man whose mirror would never weary of admiring him.

Fylan gave _____ the name of a debt. We were to put a scare into him.

We tried his front door as a start. Cain was the name we were after and it was listed as the basement apartment. We got no response. There was an office where we could have enquired but we wouldn't have wanted to trouble anyone.

_____ sized up the building, then we walked around the side. We had to climb a wall. _____ had me make a ledge with my hands and hoist him over. Then I found a trash-can and achieved the same using it.

The back of the building was more promising. _____ lifted a grate and dropped in beside some half-moon windows that looked into the basement apartment. He took off his hat but then returned it to his head and told me to pass him mine. He put his hand inside it and punched a hole in the window, then traced the frame to get rid of the remainder of the glass. He shook the hat and handed it back to me. Then he pushed his legs in the window and slipped inside.

I was pretty convinced my shoes would fit through the window—I wasn't so sure about the rest of me. Still I climbed into the trough and fit the grille back in place above my head, and started measuring myself with a small half-moon-shaped window. Feet in first, then legs, then as if I was wearing the window as a belt a couple of notches too tight, but I made it through. I had to hold my arms straight above my head and fall into the room like that. It didn't do my back much good, being bent out of shape and raked by the bottom of the window frame, and my mood wasn't in great shape either by the time I reached the floor, my feet crunching on glass, my mitts high, like I was surrendering to an empty room and _____'s grin.

I gave my shoulders a turn just to make sure I still could and _____ came over and took my hat off my head. He brushed some more glass from it and handed it back.

After we had given the apartment a once-over, _____ dragged over a high-backed chair and arranged it facing the door.

_____ told me what we were going to do to Cain. He said that we could just beat him or break his hand, and that would, doubtless, be enough to motivate him to pay his debts. I started to say that we'd beaten plenty of people, and broken enough hands and thumbs, and he interrupted, agreeing. This was why we'd always made a good team, because we understood each other, _____ said. He flipped out his knife and said that when Cain appeared we would take him and cut off his ear, and he made a slicing motion with the knife.

I thought it over and had to admit that I couldn't remember us ever having cut off an ear.

_____ sat in the chair, where he'd be the first thing Cain would see when he walked in. I would be standing behind the door, hidden from view. So I stood behind the door, and we waited.

It took some time for me to feel my legs beginning to lock into place. I stayed still. I watched _____ sitting in his chair, watching the door.

I wondered how long we would wait if we had to, whether _____ would still stare at the closed door through another day if the sun came up and the door still hadn't opened and Cain still hadn't returned. I guessed that we probably would—this was the only job we had to do.

And then it was so dark I could barely see _____—just his outline, just. I had lost all the feeling in my legs—I was half a person. We waited.

When Cain opened the door and entered the room, he was back-lit from the corridor. He was a large man, tall with long arms that hung from wide shoulders with an aspect of weighted force, like a piece of prospecting machinery. He stood facing _____ sitting in his shadow and his chair. I swung the door shut behind Cain and the light slid away like it sensed trouble. The last thing it showed was his face turned to me, a good-natured face trying to figure out what joke we were playing on him. Then the darkness had crossed him and the three of us sunk to the bottom of it.

Soon we had the lights back on, and Cain dragged into the chair. _____ pushed back his forehead—his hair was cropped too close to grab—and gave him a couple of slaps around the face. He told him to pay attention and, as he put his hand toward his pocket to get the knife, I saw for the first time that Cain was unbalanced when it came to ears.

The left was as it should have been, but above the central hollow of the right there was nothing and below it there was only a mound of flesh like drooping wax, which ended in an earlobe.

_____ had seen it too. He held the knife down by his side and looked at the half an ear. It was peculiar. We'd decided to do something, and here it was already done for us. _____ pressed a finger at the side of Cain's head, as though he was testing if it would hurt him. It didn't seem to. Cain's head bent away from the pressure, but he didn't wince.

_____ took his cigarettes from his pocket and lighted one as he inspected the missing ear. The top of the half-ear was lined with darkness that mottled and sent chubby wisps of black into the remaining pink flesh. And in the red outline of the whole ear—from when it had been whole—there was a gallows, a sickly yellow colour.

Cain looked at us both from the chair. He rubbed at the base of his back. His face went from _____ to me and back. He looked awake. He looked keen to find something to feel good-natured about. _____ drew on his smoke and told him to sing out. And when Cain's face again turned to me, for explanation _____ pushed his finger into the grisly red where Cain's ear wasn't.

45

Cain started to say something about money, and _____ said 'Nix' and prodded the ear again. 'Tell us this story.'

When Cain told it, it was from that place that people keep stories they've told so often they no longer see anything past the words they're using. The words have become shapes that they know from experience construct what they mean to reconstruct. He said how he'd been an iceman a long while, carrying ice on his shoulder wrapped in a sackcloth. He'd wear a wool shirt and a leather vest and a sackcloth would go around the ice. Except one day, not long after he started carrying ice, so he was still probably seventeen at the time, maybe eighteen, he forgot to take his sackcloth with him, and he was already slow doing his round so he couldn't go and get it.

He found another wool shirt, and draped that across his head and shoulder to give him some cover for the ice, and didn't even notice how cold he had become. He said that you were always cold carrying ice—probably the first thing he should have noticed was how quickly his head stopped feeling cold, numbed. And he said that at the end of his route the ear was yellow and, when he touched it, like it would have been happy coming clean off, if he'd been able to get a grip on it. It felt wet, like he was reaching his hand into a bucket of ice water with an ear sat in the bottom, not something attached to a head, certainly not to *his* head. And then the ear blackened and hardened, and most of it did come off.

Cain gestured with his hands, like he was sorry his story didn't have much of an ending. _____ didn't say anything, just leaned down toward him, putting his hands on the chair's armrests, and kept leaning, so far forward that Cain pressed himself into the back of the chair and had to turn his head to the side, leaving _____ staring at a missing ear, which he did. _____ didn't rush. There was no rush for us, not with our job already done.

Then _____ pushed the flat of his hand into Cain's head, pinning it to the chair, and raised his knife. Cain watched it like there was fishing line from his eye to the edge of the blade. When it had almost reached him, his body threatened to make a move, and _____'s hand widened and pushed him more firmly back. _____'s knife touched the half-ear, and slid slowly, deliberately along and down its blackened edge, tracing it like a barber shaving a well-liked customer's neck.

That night there was another card game, larger than usual. It started with five players. _____, Lydia, a Greek barber who lived in the building, an ex-buzzer called Palmer, a dog handler from the track.

And the kid, the talker, was there—Holcomb, who sank into a ball when he got a bad hand and about bust through the ceiling when he had the goods. He was on cheerful form. He made it clear that he'd just been paid, talking about it and then, when that didn't get the acclaim he

47

wanted, taking the money from his pocket and fanning it for us all to admire.

Only now that he had some money, for the first time he didn't seem to have any interest in losing it. He made himself comfortable in his chair, sitting out as many hands as he played.

One hand he folded his cards before the flop, then pulled out from under the table a small calfskin case that looked new and opened with a snap. From the case he took some wine glasses, enough for everyone at the table. A red scale curved inside each base, a wine stain. He took a bottle from the case and half-filled the glasses with whisky.

Then he sat back and swirled his glass lazily and started talking. His subject was how much he liked getting paid, and particularly how much he liked getting paid by the word. (Holcomb, it transpired, wrote stories.) He spoke for a long time about the various feelings having some money in his pocket gave him. The other players sipped at their whiskies. None of them listened.

Lydia went to smoke a black cigarette at the window and look out at the street. The apartment manager was gone and she didn't know where. If anyone at the table knew they were too kind to tell her. I sat in for her.

Holcomb reached quickly the point in his bottle and the evening where his glass butted against his mouth when he lifted it, and drops of the whisky slid down his chin, and when he set it on the table more slopped over the side. He said,

'The beautiful thing about being paid by the word is that it supplies us with an exchange rate between reality and language. Wait, no, that's getting ahead of myself, that is abrupt and ugly, a dull edge. We shouldn't allow dull and brutal things,' he said, looking at me—I guess because I was the only person still giving him the attention he wanted, 'when we speak any more than we would when we write.' I had low suited connectors in my hand.

'The beautiful thing about being paid by the word,' said Holcomb, 'is—well, let's say all my money comes from my writing and all the writing I do is paid by the word. I write for the love pulps mainly. Terrible things, too coy even to have the dignity of the earnestly seedy. Some science fiction too.

'Now obviously you could go through my apartment, and for each of my belongings you could attach a label with the cash value of that item. I paid this much for the typewriter, this much for the desk, this much for the brandy. Each word I write I get paid a nickel. Sometimes it's less than that, sometimes it's even a bit more. But let's say a nickel. If you know how many nickels I paid for something you could figure out a word that I've sold the necessary number of times to pay for that thing.

'Now we've got a new set of labels for my belongings. It's not a number and a dollar sign. The scotch is labelled "suddenly". The typewriter's got the label "lusting". There's plenty of lusting in love pulps. But the desk's even more expensive, so it's labelled with a pronoun maybe, or a conjunction. Perhaps "because" is enough to buy the desk. I see your "rugged" and raise you "wistful"!' he said and threw a couple of chips into the pot, though he'd folded the hand without even looking at his cards. _____ gave him a look and the kid pulled them back, being careful not to disturb the pile.

I folded. Only two players, _____ and Palmer, were still in the pot. Palmer had got early retirement from the force when he was photographed selling guns out the back of his prowl car. We'd met him when we had to break his hand over a small debt. _____ called a raise and dealt another card. Holcomb drew on his cigarette with a look of great concentration.

_____ took the pot and passed the deck for the dog handler, sitting on his left, to shuffle and deal.

'What's beautiful about being paid by the word,' said Holcomb, 'is that we know exactly what everyone in this room is worth.' He crossed his arms and took another drag on his smoke. 'Assuming that they're worth anything.' He was offered a card and rejected it, and the game carried on without him. I got another bum hand and folded to a low raise. From the window, Lydia said, 'What's horrible about low-rent writers being paid by the word, is that they feel the need to keep going on even when they've run out of things to say.'

'Think about how many words anyone's going to spend describing you,' Holcomb carried on, looking at her. 'Maybe your beau's composing sonnets right now instead of at a leg show or haggling prices for a lay. Could be.' Lydia threw a look at him, spat it. 'And maybe Mrs Palmer's at home right now filling notebooks with beautiful similes, pages and pages of heartfelt whimsy.'

'There ain't no Mrs Palmer,' said Palmer, though I don't think Holcomb heard him. 'Not presently, leastways.' Lydia smoked her black cigarette and looked out at the empty street however people look at things that don't mean anything.

I nearly said something to all this, but I couldn't find the words or the energy. If Lydia had been the kind to take offence I might have worked harder at it.

'Let's suppose they are! Right this moment—they're hard at work behind a pile of heretofore unexpressed affection and rhyming dictionaries. Unimportant—it doesn't matter. What I mean is, how many words would it take to plumb the depths? How many nickels before they, or anyone else who might turn their pen to the task, scraped bare the walls of the soul they set out to describe?'

The dog handler pushed in half his chips, the stub of his cigar rolling from one side of his mouth to the other. It was the most he'd moved all night. He was like an old Basset Hound which didn't get excited for much of anything lately, not since its owners had it put down. He kept his hat on at the table, the smoke from the cigar catching and then deflecting on the brim, so it tumbled like a waterfall upended.

The only others left in were me and _____. I called, _____ folded. Palmer laid another card on the table. The old dog handler didn't raise his old runny eyes, just pushed in the rest of his chips, worked his cigar with his big jaw. I called, and looked round to find Lydia had turned from the window and moved toward the game, watching as I doubled her chips, which felt good. When I'd turned my cards to show the droopy hound, I looked to her and she smiled at me, a small smile like it was something she'd whispered, so just I'd catch it. The dog handler took his jacket from the back of his chair, straightened his hat on his head, nodded to the room and left.

Holcomb watched the door close behind the dog handler. 'A paragraph and a half? Maybe two? What's that, two hundred words? Five cents a word gives us five dollars for a hundred words. So ten dollars,' he said and turned around to look at Palmer, then Lydia, then at the Greek barber. 'How much for this whole room? How much for you, loogan?' he said to me. I stood up and he backed off as if I'd pulled a gun on him, and Lydia took her seat at the table. Holcomb lighted a cigarette, trying to look casual. 'How many words for you, Box?' he said again. I filled my glass at the tap and sat and watched the game for a while longer.

I didn't even own a rod.

Neither did _____.

After he'd quit talking, Holcomb found himself in a room where all there was for him to do was lose money, but still not in a mood to do it. Losing he could do when it made him feel a victim, but the bills in his wallet were too big a cushion for him to be anything but comfortable, at least in a small stakes game like this. And he was all but incapable of winning.

If only he hadn't been so lousy at cards. It must have been bittersweet for him—a writer that easy to read.

I didn't think of that line, that's something Lydia used on him once at the table. A good one.

In the uneasy relationship between Jarecki and Danskin, we were an incursion or we were payback, depending on how you happened to approach the issue. One of Danskin's boys had got on the wrong side of Jarecki. Whether or not he knew he had wasn't a question for us.

He was called Gabriel. He had knocked around a girl— something he'd done before, but in the past it had always been one of Danskin's girls, and with Danskin, Gabriel enjoyed immunity. He didn't get that freedom with Jarecki, and this time he'd taken it out on a girl who belonged to someone who belonged to someone, who belonged to—and at the top of the chain was Jarecki, and then it becomes politics.

We took him off the street outside Danskin's club, where it would be clear that we knew exactly who he was. The club was called 'The Little Death', which is one way to bring in the crowds.

We took him to a hold-up outside the new quarter: two rooms and no neighbours.

Soon we were mainly waiting for the times when he regained consciousness. I was drinking water and _____ was throwing his knife into the wall, and Gabriel would wake cautiously and maybe feel around his mouth with his tongue, counting the missing teeth, touching the split across the edge of his lower lip.

The eye that could still blink, blinked. He moved one leg off the bed clumsily, like it was weighted. Then the other, then he stood in a push of effort. One arm was no good, but his legs could still carry him. Maybe they couldn't if he still weighed what he did a week ago, but now his ribcage was visible through the sagging armholes of his vest. He tried a slow turn of the bad arm and his shoulder resisted unevenly, like its rotation was through different thicknesses of hurt.

_____ would throw his knife a couple more times then we'd get back to the business of bouncing Gabriel off the walls.

Finally we were told to return what was left of him, and we left it back outside The Little Death, still breathing.

We were enjoying our relationship with Jarecki—it was honest work and it kept us busy. Then it stopped.

Interlude

Hector kneels, inspecting the object where it trembles, insectile, from the movement of the train. It holds one fluttering wing up in the air, and he takes it between his fingers.

It is a white matchbook with a black and red emblem reproduced on the upper-side of its one white wing. Like vertebrae in a foreshortened spine, the black ridges of the sulphur-tipped matches run half its width.

'A completely ordinary object,' Hector says, and Charles nods. 'But it feels interesting. What is interesting about it?' He tucks the wing into its place, as if he is tucking a sheet beneath a cadaver, and holds it, flat on his palm, towards Charles, who turns it on its back. The emblem seems to resemble a stain, a camouflage. Beneath it, in black type, there is an address that means nothing to either of them.

'Intrinsically,' says Charles, 'you would have to say that there's nothing. I'm sure I have its twin in my pocket right now, and if I don't I'm sure I did yesterday and I don't care much either way.'

'We're agreed that we don't find matchbooks as a rule fascinating,' says Hector.

'Yes. Not any matchbook I can remember. Not the one that might be in my pocket, not one you might buy from any pretty girl with a tray. No more interesting than the girl, or the man who dropped this matchbook, or the railing he went over. But.'

'But. We are agreed that this one has interest. A strange kind of interest. Because the interest would be of the same character if the colour of the thing was different, if the address belonged to the opposite side of its street or to a different street or city, if it was full of matches instead of half robbed of them.'

'Because the interest,' says Charles, 'is extrinsic to the matchbook.'

'It is attached to the matchbook but belongs to the man,' says Hector, 'and though we met only briefly I think we are confident the man is of little interest also.'

Sometimes, though not now, Charles despises the sound of Hector's voice. He finds it nasal and pinched, and once these qualities prickle his attention, which they occasionally do, the awareness overfills him and he finds his partner's company intolerable, to the point that he imagines committing violence against him.

Mainly though, as now, he focuses not on the pitch of his voice but on his words, and finds it not unpleasant at all, in fact he finds it deeply pleasant, soothing in the way the noise and motion of the train is soothing. His own thoughts often come to sound like Hector talking and he takes great delight in listening to the sound of his own thoughts. He coaxes Hector, 'We are confident that the man is of little interest. So.'

'So,' says Hector, 'the interest is not in the matchbook,

not even really in the man, but in his murder. This is why it is interesting: because it recently came into contact with a man who was subsequently thrown from the rear of a train and to his death. How would you describe the man? Of course, you wouldn't, is the straight answer: no one would. If you attempted it, you wouldn't be able to do much better than to say, here was a man who would be unlikely to leave any evidence of himself. Neither by the end of this train journey, nor by the end of his life. And yet what do we have?' Hector holds the matchbook up.

'Evidence,' says Charles. 'The matchbook is interesting because it has become evidence in a murder. It has become entangled in a story about a man dying violently.'

They feel interested in the matchbook.

Then, they begin to feel less interested. They've explored their interest and in this way they have exhausted or maybe exposed it.

Hector drops the matchbook back to the rattling ground and, with a foot, pushes it from the train. There are hours still to go, and even those hours account for only this journey, and not all the hours there will be in all the other journeys they take. Even if they don't take them, if they revolt from ever travelling again, they will be left only with other time, perhaps slower time, time not lulled by the movement and faded roar of a train.

Charles begins to wonder if, as well as being bored by the matchbook, there is another quality to the feeling that has settled on him like a bird too heavy for its branch.

PART 2

We were back to where all _____ had was his poker games and all I had was getting out to stretch my legs in the morning. He'd brought me nothing that didn't wear out. He was the littlest lit fuse and not attached to anything, a fizzing piece of limp, loose string.

On any day that _____ didn't disappear out, we'd go to Jarecki's club and get chased away like bad luck, told to wait. If _____ knew why there was no work for us he would have said—he would have liked to show that Fylan cared to give him the straight—but he never said, so he didn't know. Instead of going to Jarecki's or once we'd been chased away, _____ would go running after women or drinking and I'd sit in his apartment and a feeling would come over me.

The feeling was that instead of sitting in an empty room I was looking at one from outside. There was no one there, not me and also not anyone else: no one who might choose to go out the door or open a window or throw themselves from it. A whole day would pass with nothing but this feeling, which left no space for anything else but was bottomlessly empty all the same.

_____ at least had the poker games. The apartment manager had stayed absent without leave and Lydia stopped playing, and without her there I couldn't bring myself to sit at the table. I'd stay in the other room and be restless. I'd think maybe I should take to sleeping under parked cars and hope for the best.

One morning lying on the table with the abandoned cards there was a magazine. It was a pulp with the word 'Astonishing' on the front. The cover showed a cliff, and by the edge of it a machine about the size of two cars piled on top of each other. And on the far side of the machine, his back to you, was a man in a white lab coat, waving a fiery torch, and coming at him through sick yellow fog a gang of skinny, hairless, naked men, shiny wet. Naked but with a smooth curve where one shouldn't be. The scientist's torch didn't seem to be discouraging them from getting closer to the machine. It said 'Traveller Through Time!'

I looked inside the magazine. The story that matched the cover had Holcomb's name at the top: he must have brought it to show off some of the words he'd been paid for. With nothing else to do I read it, and after I read it I couldn't make much sense of that picture. There was no cliff-top or torch anywhere in the story. There was a race of almost human creatures, but Holcomb didn't call them like the sweating, bald things in the picture. In fact, he hardly called them at all.

The story starts with the machine arriving. Wait, that's not quite right. It starts with there being a strange, 'violent' kind of movement like the machine is there, but it's not. Then the machine is there—in the middle of this empty plain. Well it starts with an empty plain, then the machine arrives—first there's the violent blur, and then the machine is there and the scientist gets out of it and looks around the 'stricken landscape', though you don't know at that point that he's a scientist.

First there's nothing, just—nothing—and then there's this movement, this violent—well, first there's nothing just this 'desolate, stricken landscape' and then there's, firstly there's the sense of movement, as if 'of a candle being observed' but 'only at the furthest point to which its flicker reaches, as it is buffeted by an unremitting wind'. And then the machine appears. Well, the machine is part of the movement, part of the blur, and then the scientist, the man, gets out of the machine, only once the blur has settled and the machine has 'appeared, both instantly and gradually—as an abrupt shout leaves behind itself a series of echoes that merge and vanish, like ripples after the sinking of the stone', then the scientist, or the man, gets out. And he looks around and he laughs. Then these things appear. Though he laughs for a long time before that, I should have said.

First there is a 'desolate, stricken landscape', a 'great vastness' and not much else, then there's this 'impression of violent motion in the middle of the plain where previously had been nothing, not even any of the . . .' I should have mentioned that scattered across the plain there are 'large, dying' shrubs.

There is a 'desolate, stricken landscape; large, dying

shrubs the single feature, embedded regularly throughout its great absence. In plains roiled by centuries of wind and rain, they were dying in large unmourned patches, shedding grey thorns from their great mangled bodies. Into this forbidding scene, there appeared what would have seemed a most unusual visitation, had there been any attentive eye to witness it: a sudden but lingering blur where before there had been nothing. From nothing a large grey mass appeared, a blur with an outline that was indistinct but unshifting, as though the contents of some unseen division were being agitated by a powerful force.'

This blur, this 'mass', 'resolved itself into the shape of a machine, the metal skeleton of a box with a man at its heart'.

After what was neither an age nor a moment, the man climbed unsteadily from his seat in the machine and looked around the landscape without expression—whether of surprise, disgust, horror or delight. He seemed, as a man, the match of the wasteland he stared into. Until his lips parted and a laugh, both joyless and triumphant, climbed from him, and kept rising, a bitter witness to the death sentence of a ravaged world. As he leaned on his strange machine and laughed, tears glommed to his grey, crazed eyes and fell in the dust by his feet, already the colour of the dry dirt on which they stood, and still he laughed on and on, until his voice cracked and gave, and a rasp was all that the landscape swallowed.

Then, as the man's voice seemed to have passed the final reaches of his strength, another noise arose.

This dull, regular sound came from neither the man nor his contraption. It gripped the man tight. He seemed for the first time more than the mysterious metal machine that had delivered him. He had become an animal, its senses overwhelmed.

The sound began as if a dismal echo of his laugh, as though the sound of the madman on his knees had been taught to the broken strings of old pianos and the crushed throats of clarinets, and they compelled to repeat it.

From one of the large plants there came a figure.

Small and grotesque, its mouth wide, emitting the troubling noise, or rather a share of the noise, it advanced on him.

Its appearance adjusted the man's conception of the plant from which it had emerged. These plants, which everywhere blighted the landscape, and which he had assumed stood no taller than himself, he now understood to be larger than the tallest tree he had ever in the whole of his life encountered. And as he turned towards another, a dozen more figures emerged from it, all the match of the first, all with their mouths open, cruelly imitating his own cruel laugh.

As they advanced their heads turned incessantly from side to side, the creatures surveying each other then turning again to the true man suddenly amongst them, and then away again. And with every steady turn of their heads, they came closer.

While the noise they gave and the movement of their heads was constant and smooth, their gait was quite the opposite: a jerky movement, as though they kept confronting and climbing an obstacle, though it was an obstacle they carried with them in their own godless design.

The man watching their approach was still. If his laughter before had been that of a man who felt no horrors were unknown to him, his humanity crawled anew at the sight of these greatly changed creatures. But he had no strength in him to move, or make so much as a noise.

Until a hand clasped his wrist.

Now he was amid tens of the creatures who grasped at him, while more approached. And in the alertness of terror he saw the hand that held his forearm and was appalled.

The palm was a bloated ball, as though swollen with disease, ill fit for any purpose he could imagine, and from this ball of flesh there sprouted fingers that resembled vines more than they did anything human. They were extremely long with a great many points of articulation. The touch was repellent, but still he did nothing. The Time Traveller's eyes moved from the spindled boil of a hand to the dark gawping mouth of the creature, which carried the awful sound into his face on a rotten wind.

And from beside him came the same noise, and his face was blasted by another vulgar breath and another hand wrapped itself around him, between his arm and his side.

More of the creatures now laid hands on the Time Traveller, wrapping the vines of their fingers around each of his legs, and the first to have reached him placed its other around his neck, exploring the edge of his mouth.

Gripped by the long fingers of a dozen bulbous hands, abused by the cacophonous, foul sound of a hundred and more hideous voices, the Traveller remained still, only his eyes betraying his terror. It was as if the grip of the cold grey flesh was a horror endured without hope of it ever ending, without duration; he was a prisoner held within an unspeakable moment, bound by wet fingers that tied knots around him like the cold, hard ropes on the deck of a ship.

Suddenly the man shrieked back at the wailing creatures. And he tore violently at their hands. And as a glass might draw vibrations from those glasses around it, the piercing shriek spread from his human mouth to their all too different mouths.

As the Traveller clawed and tore at the hands he was unaware of the violence he was doing. It was only once he had almost freed himself, when almost all of the creatures' voices had turned to a shriek, that the thought reached him of how weak the grip that held him had been, and how awful had been the effect of the blows he had thrown to save himself.

When the sights of his own struggle finally reached him, they were of long hard fingers being snapped and torn; hideous faces being split open by each punch as if they were soft, rotted fruit and collapsing on themselves like wet card. So great was the violence exhibited on the creatures that the Traveller imagined it a form of psychic terror he exercised against them, the manifestation of his revulsion at the touch of the swollen grey hands, which snapped and bled and withdrew badly frayed and hanging in pieces at unbearable angles. His fury at the ugly, braying figures introduced new geometric forms into them with great force: one face and then another suddenly dented almost in half, as if struck by a chisel. In this way he made sense of a brutality that seemed impossible from the tired swings and pushes of his limbs, but matched perfectly the vehemence of his will.

Screeching and bleeding, the creatures' heads recoiled, and from the great darkness of its throat one of the beasts, a monster with half a shattered eye, gurgled sibilantly and sprayed a muddy dart of fluid across the Time Traveller's clothes, then another did the same, until they were all spraying foul liquid across his neck and face, and only his eyeglasses prevented it from entering his eyes.

It was this barrage that finally propelled the Time Traveller back towards the machine, which, when he had stepped from it, he could not have conceived of ever entering again. Only this God-forsaken place could force him back into the contraption. This dead earth, with these monstrous creatures slinging venom, with their hard, weak flesh, the puppet shells that cracked and tore with such ease.

But now, moved by horror, disgust and a care for his own life he had thought lost, the Time Traveller wiped at his spectacles and started the machine.

For a moment, as the edges of the machine began to flicker, he took satisfaction in seeing the creatures nearest to it torn apart, the creature with the half-eye that was staggering and clutching towards him being reduced to a bloody spray.

This was an instant's pleasure.

And then his own body felt as if turned to stone and, for the second time, his hell began.

Now, beside the machine, specks of dark blood clumped and inexpertly bound themselves with grey flesh into a creature with half an eye that moved as though tugged from behind. The other creatures also retreated, as a low wave upon reaching its furthest point slips back into the sea. And now withdrawing with them from the machine came the Time Traveller himself. He watched as his own image backed into the creatures and with great, decorative contortions enmeshed itself in a mound of greyness, bound by the clutching monsters.

The Traveller in the machine made to turn away, but his head remained facing the knot of bodies with himself at its centre, remained as the minutes passed and from this mound individual creatures extricated themselves and loped away, their gait even more awkward and ungainly than it had been when time proceeded untampered. And as the world began to retrace its unhurried steps and the creatures moved away, it was into a thickening white fog, which fell all around the machine. Until finally nothing at all was visible beyond the confines of the machine, as if the Time Traveller was a caged bird in a stage magician's trick, and a sheet had been laid over him. Horror in torrents took the mind of the Time Traveller. He forced his arm towards the lever that would halt the machine, knowing that it would be many, many years before it achieved even the slightest movement. Knowing that, should he blink, he would watch the eclipse form for thousands of years.

Knowing that whatever the extreme sloth of his body that made his glorious invention function, his mind would be conscious of the passing of the years, the millions of years, between this and his own time.

He might have known the exact number of years—from a small change in darkness he had come to distinguish between, so he imagined, day and night—but at various points in his outward journey madness had robbed him of the figure. And now he waited for madness to come again, the only confessor, saint or nurse that could reach him in the rigid trap of his own frame.

For days, weeks, years and millennia, awake and without reprieve, as his mind sat in solitude for longer than any civilisation had ever survived, for longer than the legacy of species, or the formation of rocks, the Traveller's mind sang a song it had written long before the end of its last journey through this frozen hell, and had forgotten and rewritten many times, and had reduced until it was one phrase thought in all the pitches the Traveller was able to conceive it, a childhood phrase told the Time Traveller by his brother as a boy when they were at play, which was actually combat, in which the older boy had forced him to the ground and, with the conqueror's self-delight which even the boy beneath his heel admired as heroic, said, 'I am an explorer and all this land is mine forever.' And the Time Traveller prayed for madness or death, 'And all this land is mine forever.'

That's how the story ended: 'all this land is mine forever'.

It would have been a better read with more talking in it, but it had still passed the time.

With _____ out somewhere chasing distractions, I read the rest of the magazine, but I hustled through it without interest. Instead I came back to Holcomb's story. I examined the drawing on the front cover, and then I read it again.

I read it that whole day, and kept reading it, read it until I was just reading the last section, with the Traveller in his machine, frozen, waiting through the years backwards after waiting through them forwards.

I read it enough that it seeped out of the story. When I thought about _____ sitting in Cain's chair waiting while the room darkened around him, I also thought about him sitting in the Traveller's machine, and he was waiting through days and days, without moving so much as his eyes. _____ was thrown from a moving car into my life and as he tumbled at me it was the lurch of one of the creatures and I recoiled at his grip. I lay on _____'s bed and pulled the bedsheets over my face and I thought of the bird in the magic trick, the world fading to white around the Traveller until there was nothing he could see except the steady changing of the light.

I fell asleep there, because _____ woke me—giddy.

We were summoned.

I took the magazine with me.

Not Jarecki's gambling joint this time—it was a club we went to, like Danskin's Little Death, somewhere to see a leg show. It had been a picture house, then Jarecki bought it cheap after a cop was shot there. The circumstances hadn't been good for the cop, but few enough people knew the details that the force only had to crack a few heads to claim the moral high ground and shut the place down.

Jarecki had ripped out the screen and the seats. He got tables made that accounted for the slope of the floor. He got chairs that didn't, but put his waitresses in outfits that pretty much guaranteed no one would notice. And twice a night and three times on weekends there was an elaborate dance number on stage, and the rest of the time there were still leg kicks and sweet young souls singing their hearts out. It was a swell place, and swells filled it. The new club thrived—and Danskin's Little Death didn't suffer, pretty girls being one of those industries that makes its own rules, demand-wise.

I sat backstage while _____ talked with Fylan about things that didn't concern me, which is how _____ would sometimes describe all the things that concerned me that he didn't want me to have a say in.

The only thing going on was practice, and even practice was taking a break. The girls came through, standing and sitting, rubbing sore thighs, tugging each other's hair. They had on little or no make-up, hair tied back, all twelve within an inch of the same height, all wearing show shoes that glittered and their own clothes that didn't.

One of the girls was being teased by the rest. They took turns with snide remarks about her as their attention and their cigarettes allowed.

She had been called Diamond, but had changed her name to Dorothy when she started dancing. The other girls couldn't believe that her parents had given her this gift, this perfect name for the sort of stage they kicked their heels on, and she had changed it. This is what they were teasing her about, but why they were teasing her was obvious. It was because when all these girls walked into a room, she was the one you saw. She had darkly shining, hooded eyes, and there was something about her, even in the loose, ill-fitting clothes she'd worn to practice, that made your imagination slip its leash, whether or not you knew you had one. Eleven other beautiful girls, and against her they were all flashlights at a summer picnic.

Dorothy watched this scene, the backstage teasing, like she was waiting for her cue. She had one leg crossed over the other and held a cigarette between two steepled fingers, while she rubbed a thread of dropped tobacco between two of the fingers on her other hand and looked twice as good as breakfast.

Eventually the other girls had all laughed themselves hoarse with jealousy. Dorothy put out her cigarette and, before she stood, slapped her hands against her legs. It was a man's gesture, and then as soon as she was standing there was no trace of it. She was deliberate—she could have been on screen or painted on canvas. When she began to speak it was over the last of the chatter, but it sounded like a long silence had just been broken.

As she talked she told the other girls some ugly truths, and she didn't care that they hurt. And you'd have wanted her to tell you ugly hurtful things too, just so she'd look you in the eye while she did it and you'd get to know that thoughts of you were moving those lips.

She told them how it had never mattered what her name was. She pronounced each of the other girls' names in turn, and made each sound boring and leaden, and you could tell they hated themselves for not being able to think a bad thought about this Dorothy's posture, or her looks, or her tall, firm body, or her callous, impeccable mouth. She told them that they needed their names to get noticed. She didn't. When she'd grown up in her own little no-horse town, a big-city photographer approached her on the street, asking her to model for him, and she'd said no because he dressed cheap. Would they have done that? Wasn't it the sort of thing they dreamed would ever happen to them in their own no-horse towns?

She'd been pacing slowly, her calf getting taut as each heel placed itself on the ground, first her left leg then her right then the left again in a way that demanded constant attention. And now she came over to me and sat on my lap and tangled her legs around each other and gave a yawn that stretched her out from top to tail.

'I knew I was going to be here tonight, out front and centre, even then,' she said. She looped her arm as far across my shoulders as it would go and swung her dangling legs playfully. She'd made me into a prop for her, into her stage. It was exciting. 'I love you all, and I need you all. Because a room is just so boring without wallpaper, don't you think?' She took a long drag on her cigarette and let the smoke spill from her nostrils and lazily unfurl into my eyes.

A weary man with his sleeves rolled up came and clapped his hands at them, until they all put out their lights and went back to practice, eleven cute little tricks and one name for the playbill.

Then _____ reappeared, looking aggrieved.

He patted an envelope impatiently against his thigh, jerked his head toward the exit with a brisk whistle between his front teeth and I followed him out. In the street _____ pulled the lip of the envelope back with a finger to show me the contents and flicked through them with his thumb. The envelope was full of notes—twenties mainly but fifties too, enough to keep us going for a month or more. He took out about half of the pile and handed it to me.

He told me I could go get a coffee, take in a show. I could go bark at cars for all he cared. Jarecki had said there wasn't any work going, wouldn't be anything for us to do for a while. This was to tide us over. Then he pulled his pack of cigarettes from his jacket pocket and gave a sharp twitch of his hand, as if he had been about to toss the packet into the air and immediately thought better of it, so that one of the pills jumped half clear of the rest.

I looked through the money he'd given me a couple of times and told him I thought I'd go get a steak.

So the two of us went and sat in a place and ordered two rare steaks from the waiter, with one beer and one glass of water to go with them.

_____ finished the beer as soon as it hit the table. As he ordered a second, we got the smell of the butter and the onions hitting the pan, and we moved to sit at the counter in front of the grill, so we could get more of it. _____ was having the onions with his steak, I was just having the steak, and it was good and properly rare.

After we'd finished _____ took a third beer and I had one too, though I don't drink beer often. I don't like the feeling of being drunk because I don't like not being able to choose not to be drunk any longer, but I could see some value in it, in a day when there was nothing else to be done. And when that beer was done we had another, and ordered some more onions, not to eat, just so we'd get the smell again as they were cooked.

It was maybe four in the afternoon, but we were both tired, the sort of tiredness you get from doing nothing, the sort of tiredness you get if you watch other people exhaust themselves.

Back at the apartment we brushed our teeth at the sink. _____ is more thorough than me and I was done first. I reached forward with a glass to fill it at the tap, and almost got it filled with the last of _____'s spitting, and we apologised, each to the other.

Then _____ got into the bed and I lay down on the mattress on the floor and we slept through the day, which was the Tuesday, and on Wednesday we threw cards from a deck across the room into _____'s hat, _____ sitting in his vest and shorts.

For those three days having nothing to do felt like ease and calm, and _____'s company was almost good enough to keep, but through the Thursday, while _____ threw more cards and smoked cigarettes, I had the feeling my skin was tightening, like someone had found a crank that fitted in the base of my neck, in a socket hidden by the line of my hair, and was turning it, and with each gear half an inch of skin was threaded into my spine, until I was a ten-pound soul squeezed into a five-pound sack.

Maybe _____ had a tightening crank of his own. By the

Thursday morning he took to drinking. He cursed Jarecki and he cursed Fylan, and he said that they were lucky if he didn't take their little city from them and grind it under his heel. He said that a man who couldn't at any moment point to a dozen necks he'd like snapped was a man without imagination who didn't deserve to be in charge of a poem, let alone a city. And if Jarecki had necks that needed snapped and he wasn't sending them our way then—

But who knows what then, because _____'s irritation made the glass he had in his grip explode into pieces. He screamed curses at me and Jarecki and the glass and the city for half of a count to 100. 100 being the number I had chosen to count to before I popped him in the jaw and we would see where that took us. At fifty he went quiet and together we picked up the fragments of the glass. _____ got himself another and drank with renewed concentration.

He was well passed out when the writer, the Astonishing Holcomb, came to the door.

As I opened the door to Holcomb, all the thinking I had done on his story came back to me, and it took me a moment to get out what I had to say, which was that _____ was passed out drunk.

He waited longer than he had to before he replied. He hung a second of silence out in which to look at me like a son of a bitch—a second of sneering judgement on the time it had taken me to say my part. I thought of the carefully posed way he smoked cigarettes at the card table, and thought again how maybe I ought to put his teeth down his throat.

'I was hoping I could buy you a coffee, Box,' he said. Then his eyes broke from me and he looked like just the scrawny kid in a suit he was, and scared too. 'I bought a train ticket.' He lifted it out of the pocket of the jacket he was carrying slung over his arm and waved it. 'To get out of town. I was on my way to the station when it occurred to me that you might be able to help me.'

He was licked with sweat, it bloomed out from the arm-pits of his shirt and out from the sunken middle of his boy's chest. There wasn't any joke in his eyes, there wasn't the superior little brain that sneered at you across a hand of poker, just a timid child. He returned the ticket and pulled back on his hair. I told him I'd come and get a coffee.

In the coffee joint he sat, then just about turned a som-ersault squirming to see the door. 'Do you mind if we exchange seats?' he said. 'Recently I like being able to see who's coming.'

I stood up and he cowered like he hadn't just asked a favour. Then he skittered round the far side of the table into my place. He took a flask from his jacket and a guilty swig from the flask, worried the teacher might see him and tell him off. He put on a pair of big, wire-rimmed glasses I'd never seen him wear. 'Not much point being able to see the door if I can't tell who's opened it.' Then:

'I wondered,' he said, 'I wondered, Box, if you had any spare time. If you were at a loose end at all.'

I nodded. I was a handful of loose and frayed and itching ends.

We sat in silence for a while. He looked to be thinking. Nerves jogged him in his seat like he was rattling along in a train carriage. He didn't know where to put his hands until we had two coffees, then he clung to his like it was a ladder over a snake-pit.

'I'm in some trouble,' he said. 'There is a man who quite wants to kill me.' He laughed as if this was an embarrassing story he could hardly believe himself. 'At least, he told me he does, and I've started to worry that he might be serious. As I said, I'd made the decision to get on a train and leave the city, but a thought took me and brought me to your door.'

I mentioned how it was _____'s door he'd come to.

'Yes, but I was relieved when you answered it. To be honest, his presence never does much to make me feel safer, somehow.' He smiled and took a drink of his coffee. 'That's what I need, someone who can make me feel safer, until this difficulty has found some kind of resolution.' The coffee or the flask or the conversation must have been comforting him because he no longer rattled in his seat. 'This is not a situation where I need someone to crack a case by tracking down leads and figuring out the angles. I need some muscle to sit dumb and close at hand, so that if this man who wants to kill me appears, you can deal with him.'

The fear in him had begun to creep away and in its place the conceited poker player was being reassembled. He started to describe the man and the nature of his difficulty and I told him I didn't care. It knocked him back five minutes: he was just a small boy in glasses again, scared for his neck. He went quiet and sat in prayer or otherwise distracted by the table.

To pull him out of it and get on with something I asked if he had money. He scrambled a pile of it out of his pocket, and I let him count some out. When it seemed enough to be starting with, I took it.

He spent the walk to the tram knitting back together his awful personality. He talked a little about how it would have been ridiculous for him to leave town—that he'd never allow himself to be bullied from his home. He talked about the cleverness of this new arrangement he had made with me, and I got the impression that he felt that either I or the whole city should have been carrying him on our shoulders. I wondered whether _____ might have come to and sobered up yet, and decided with a little regret that probably not.

We rode the tram to the far end of the line going south. His building stood on the far corner from the stop, along-side a phone booth. It was dark brick, with small windows: it looked like a fort. Holcomb's place was on the second floor and he quietened down again when we went in, as if he was ashamed, though there wasn't much of anything there. If he had fled town all there would have been left of him was a minimum of furniture spread across two small rooms, piles of books that spilled across the floor or stood without resolve in stacks, some empty bottles in one corner arranged like skittles in an alley and, on the desk: a typewriter in a black case that made it appear tank-like, two stacks of paper, a cheap lamp, and some kind of pitted, copper-coloured metal ball the size of a grapefruit.

All of the windows were on the far wall and looked directly onto the brick face of the neighbouring building, which had taken as much as a half-step back to give Holcomb room to breathe.

He had me help him pull his desk away from the wall. He took the chair around it so he would be facing into the room, sat, spun the typewriter on its stomach to face him and removed the case, then fed the machine a sheet of paper. Then he set to write, and on the basis that I'd taken some money to watch him, I sat down on a sunken brown couch and watched him.

He tapped a few keys gingerly so he wouldn't wake anyone or disturb the sheet of paper. He got up, smoked a cigarette at the window, then went back to the desk. He tugged at his hair and his face and his tie and his shirt-sleeves like he was hoping to pick words out of them.

I thought the way he approached his work was slow going, but there was also about it something placid. He seemed to need to reach a state of peace beneath his empty bottles and gaze of the bricks through the windows. He built a church, his head hung heavy on his boy's shoulders, and his eyes darkened, and I began to feel as if I was following him out of thought, so I had little sense of the time that had passed when he shouted at me, 'I can't even begin to work if you keep staring at me!' He stormed round the desk. He opened a drawer, his back to me, and, saying as loud as he could dare himself, 'You dumb, rattle-mouthed loogan,' he retrieved a magazine and threw it at my head. 'There,' he said. 'If you need something to keep you occupied, there's that.' And he took to his typewriter again.

The magazine was another Astonishing edition. The cover for this one had a small green alien boarding a streetcar: he wore a big glass bulb of a space helmet and he was having to stand on the tips of his spaceboots to pay the driver for the ride. No one in the city seemed surprised by his small greenness, his spaceboots, space helmet, his big eyes or balloon of a head. The driver was delighted to have him on board.

I flicked through, and near the back I found a story with Holcomb's name attached to it. It was shorter than his Traveller in Time and had nothing to do with the alien on the cover.

Holcomb himself was beginning to peck a hesitant drumbeat out of his typewriter.

I read the story about the streetcar-riding alien. It was about friendly little green men landing on earth and taking up as tourists. The earthlings are shocked at first, but we grow accustomed, and everyone's happy to have them because they pay their way and they don't get under anyone's feet.

Only then they start getting interested in strange shows. A group of these aliens go and watch them give a guy the chair. They take pictures during and clap politely once they've done burning him. Then they start crowding round whenever there's a car accident. And soon this is all they're interested in. Suicides jumping from windows, knife fights outside gin joints, mishaps on building sites: interested crowds of little green aliens gather round like it's a peepshow.

Then a group of big shots—the chief of police, the mayor, some captains of industry—are all gathered together, talking this through in an office high over a city where fires burn. They start saying how maybe there are more car crashes than there used to be, and more suicides and more knife fights too. Isn't that quite the thing? Only just as they start to get a hold on the corners of this thought they get sour with each other and an argument breaks out. One of them starts bitching to himself about his lousy family while he knocks back whisky and gives the ground the evil eye, the rest poke each other in the chest and raise their voices. They start throwing fists. The chief of police pounds a captain of industry to pieces on the corner of his desk. The mayor grabs an official mayoral letter opener and slices his own secretary through the stomach, then takes one in the chest from a revolver that another captain of industry has pulled out of his sock. The unhappy family man breaks his bottle and uses it to tear out his own wrists, then finishes the job by throwing himself through the window. And outside there's a floating group of little green men, taking pictures and clapping.

It was a pretty good one.

Holcomb kept pecking away and no one arrived with the intention of pulling his throat out, so I kept reading—about an asylum for lunatics and a strange experiment, and more aliens, and cosmic rays that made the whole planet brainy for a single year. Eventually I got to Holcomb's story. 'A Strange Kind of Suicide' it was called. It was shorter than his other, the one about the creatures, but not as short as it could have been. There were maybe two bits in the whole story that you needed, the rest was dead weight.

It was another about a scientist, and Holcomb spent his time telling you how good-looking the scientist is, and how brilliant. The scientist begins the story by meeting a friend of his, a knockout frail who's obviously hung up on him, except he's so distracted by being brilliant he doesn't even notice it. And she's not the only one. Even on the way to meet her he's setting hearts on fire—there's one girl who sells cigarettes and another who doesn't do anything but fall in love with scientists on the far sidewalk. The guy is a hymnal for every woman who lays eyes on him, but he's only interested in the machine he's working on.

The machine sounded a lot like the machine in the other story—it's a metal cage the scientist has to climb inside, and it flickers when it gets turned on, only there's no sitting frozen in the seat, or grey, spitting creatures, and this time for his machine to work, the scientist has to think in a particular way. He has to think with a kind of 'drifting contemplation', which gives the machine its charge. Holcomb calls it like a gas leak ahead of an explosion: unnoticeable, but containing a great energy.

But Holcomb hasn't got his scientist into the machine yet. Not just because the scientist's too busy ignoring frails: he is afraid of his machine. He's never worried about dying before, but he thinks that now he has made this machine he could be 'the single most important figure in the world—the world of the past and of the future, as much as of the world he felt fairly sure was still outside his window'. His death would 'therefore be of epochal significance'. Besides, he seems to think that anything that goes wrong might not just be the end of him, but of a lot else too. He is a little wary of starting a machine that could destroy existence.

This is starting to take almost as long as Holcomb made it. What's important is that he has an idea to make sure the machine is safe, so he rushes back to it (the knockout frail is left, staring hungrily at empty space). He works at his machine with strange tools, and by referring to pages in 'a notation comprehensible only to the scientist'. When he is done, he has attached a safety device to tell him if his machine is safe or if it will destroy the planet: a little metal flag, hinged at the base.

That's the take of it all, out of a lot of talking about his childhood, and how the machine's meant to work and how the blue of his eyes catches the light.

After all that the 'scientist climbed into the machine', 'steadied his resolve' and began to think in his state of 'drifting contemplation', and he 'placed his hand on the lever that might change the world, or ruin it'.

And he waited for a sign, with a certainty in his waiting that no spiritual man had ever achieved. With a stomach-less, throat-less peace he waited, and as it threatened to become almost unbearable, a dark ball of unease growing within his head fed by his drifting thoughts and beyond the capacity of his skull to contain it, the signal he had been waiting for arrived, an advance party's cry that it was safe to proceed: the metal flag *turned to the left* with a small but uncanny certainty, guided by an invisible force.

The sign had been given: the machine was safe. He found himself pulling on the lever with the same mech-anised resolve.

The machine that encased him buzzed, and seemed almost to flicker, as though the world had something in its eye and was blinking this thing that should have been real and steadfast in and out of existence.

And then it was over. And he sat in the same seat, in the same room. But everything was changed.

It turns out, he's travelled into the future—though only by a couple of hours. He consults clocks he keeps around the room to confirm this, including clocks that work by dripping water or trickling sand. Holcomb spends a lot of time convincing the guy that he has succeeded. The thing that makes him buy it, persuades him he isn't being rooked, is that through the window he can see it's now dark, when it wasn't before. He's happy about this, at length.

The one thing he doesn't think of is, maybe the machine just made him pass out for a couple of hours and all he's invented is a blackjack the size of a cigarette stand. But he hasn't, anyway. He's the first time traveller. He carries on being happy about it.

Then he remembers the metal flag. He returns to the machine and reaches for it, which unlike the rest of the machine is still flickering.

This is the second bit of the story that it seems worth keeping.

He reached to the metal flag to give the signal. This was his plan; this, in a sense, he had already done. Moving the flag now, at any time in the next hour or more, he had calculated, would cause—had, in fact, caused—the flag to move on the machine in the past, where he sat waiting to begin his journey. The machine had taken him into the future; he had installed this mechanism, this means for communicating into the past.

This was the signal, and also a proof. It showed that the scientist's success was two-fold, he had taken the reins of time and he could steer it backwards with all the ease with which he had driven it forward. It allowed him to alert himself, before he operated the machine for the first time, that his attempt would be a success, and a safe success at that. When he saw the movement of the flag in that other time he would (he knew, because he remembered) mechanically pull at the lever and journey forward.

But as he reached to give the signal, he hesitated (had he hesitated before?) and considered, with a thrum of compassion or selfishness, what it would mean for the scientist that had been him, now sitting two hours in the past, holding on to the lever, waiting for the metal flag to move.

He would see the signal and launch himself forward, into—well into what exactly? Launch himself forward in time, and into the scientist now sitting with tentative hand outstretched.

Wouldn't that be a kind of death? Not as grand or important a death as he had been contemplating before, not the death of the only person to have challenged the strictness of the beat to which time, relentless, marched. But the death of someone to whom he felt a more than familial closeness: a strange kind of suicide.

If, on the other hand, he left the hammer untouched and the signal un-given, then soon there would be two of him: one who propelled himself forward, and another who allowed the current simply to carry him.

Give the signal and these two individuals would be confounded together and there would remain only one.

His hand withdrew. The eerie flicker of the hammer subsided and passed.

Unsure whether to leave, to hide, to stay: he waited.

He noticed, in the bed, in the corner of the small room, a figure he recognised, sleeping restlessly.

It felt like the story had ended as soon as Holcomb had written the number of words the magazine would give him nickels for, and never mind that so many of the words he'd written had been about the wrong things. Or as if the story had just ended when it hit the edge of the page.

But after I'd read to the end of the magazine, and gone through the advertisements too and spent some more time with the little alien boarding the streetcar, Holcomb's story stuck around, the same as his other one had. It made me busy with thoughts. It put a slide and sidestep in my head.

I lay down on the couch with my hat over my eyes. I lay there with my mind, the two of us thinking about what it would mean to live in the story, where anything you might try you could know ahead of time if it was the right thing to do. What would hit a dead-end and leave you throwing cards into a bucket, what would lead on and on, easy and good: you could look at a dreary performance and name it a rehearsal, and that would make all things possible.

*

I woke from a content sleep with Holcomb filling the world like he was leaning over my pram. 'Box,' he said, 'wake up,' shaking at my shoulder. 'I'm going through to bed. You should just sleep where you are in case our friend tries the door in the night.'

I looked at him in a way that apparently didn't communicate anything. 'Good night,' he said, and left.

It took a few restless hours to get back to sleep.

A phone call woke us in the morning. While Holcomb spoke with the careful secrecy of someone who imagines newshawks everywhere, I went to the desk drawer where he had found the magazine. There was a small pile: I took one more and put it with the alien tourist and the cliff-top machine in my coat pocket. At some point the copper ball had moved position on his desk. Maybe he juggled it when he was stuck for ideas.

When he was done with his phone conversation he chased me out of the apartment with a day the next week when he wanted me to deliver myself back, ready to serve. The look I gave must have meant something on this occasion, because he stopped shooing and went back to his timid, beaten self. He pressed some bills in my hands until I'd agreed I'd be back. What in the phone call had convinced him he was safe until the middle of the week, I couldn't say. Maybe his murderer was away, yachting.

I dragged my heels all the way to _____'s. I wasn't

93

looking forward to the two of us dealing with our foul boredom together.

But when I got to the apartment, I found _____ already dressed. He was flattening his hair with pomade and wearing a necktie. He'd shaved for the first time since before we'd had our steaks.

He told me to get dressed and sharpen up, Jarecki had been in touch and we were going to need some of our senses—we weren't just taking our hats for a walk. I shaved and dressed. _____'s being so dapper made me look at my own suit, and there was a rip by the right shoulder where the stitches at the seam had given. I put my arm out in a slow, lazy right hook and the split widened like a grinning mouth.

We walked toward the new quarter of the city while the sun was still low in the sky, sending long shadows at us. The last mile was through what had once been a nice suburb. A place where you could free the kids with an untroubled mind, and while they were playing in the street, maybe take a dive beneath the hood of the family car, get some sun and a bit of grease on your skin. But a bad surgery had given it a new type of building, taller and sometimes neon-fronted, and some of these were pawnshops and poolrooms. As we walked down the empty street, ahead of us were the one-storey homes with attached lawns and mortgage worries, and at our side, approaching with us, the city came creeping in with everything you didn't want to get involved in or you wouldn't have moved out to the suburbs.

And as the city jostled at the good people of this suburb from one side, on their other was the new quarter, ugly and hostile because it was exposed and unmade, like a skeleton hung with skin the way a coat hangs on a hat stand. It had only been half built, and now it was leaving.

Mixers and scaffolds had moved in, and men with clipboards and deadlines to meet. Together they started to make the shell of a neighbourhood, which was going to be filled with wiring and water flowing through pipes, the healthy guts of a place. Then the money had stopped because the main investor had gone to jail. He was what they call a man of means, so if he was unlucky he might have spent as much as a whole night inside, but not so long the mice would remember him. It was enough for him, anyway, judging by how quick he hustled out of the city. And with him gone, work on the new quarter dried up.

We had to move out of the road for a frame house being dragged away on wheels.

We carried on into the half-made city.

With a couple more sections of floor and maybe a few more panes of glass you would have been happy to call it a room. _____ said that this was it, we were here, but his voice disappeared into the holes in the walls. He went and pulled a folding metal chair from behind a tarp which was protecting the dignity of a pile of dirt. The chair's voice as he scraped it across the concrete floor was a lot clearer than his had been.

He set the chair up beside a window that was just a ten-inch-thick and five-foot-square absence of wall. I went looking for another chair, but without luck.

_____ had taken a small pair of binoculars from somewhere and was using them to peer out the window, his neck extended forward as if someone was holding a lighted cigar to the back of his head. He had a small notepad on his knee and a pencil between his teeth.

I looked out the window. There were two sidewalks but no blacktop on the road that split them. Opposite was another hollow, unfinished building, this one taller and weakly impressive, its stucco flourishes making it look like a small courthouse. It felt good that in this derelict place these marks of nobility made that building more ridiculous than ours.

After an hour of standing, I took the working end of a snapped brush from the corner of the room and cleaned as much of the dirt and dust as I could from the concrete floor in front of the window and sat down by _____'s feet. He was still leaning attentively forward. When he had the binoculars hanging on the tether around his neck you could see the impressions of the eyepieces in his face. They were deep and red.

Sitting on the floor, my view out the window was angled

so I could see only the top half of the official-looking build-ing. Whatever _____ was watching for, all I could see were rain gutters and a whole lot of sky. I was trusting that if anything happened he'd let me know, and I'd be able to take an active part in this thing we were involved with.

It stopped raining after a while and the clouds became occasional instead of a mass.

_____ took a couple of tongue sandwiches from his pocket and handed me the smaller one. I sat with it a while and watched as the bread slowly uncreased itself from the journey, then ate it.

One cloud looked like maybe a fraction of the turn of an ankle going into a high-heeled shoe. Another looked like the rear of a crashed car. Another like the bottom of a pair of cactuses, like it was a part of a much bigger scene in a western. The sky underneath it was reddening so I guess that was the western's desert, although the timing and the redness weren't quite right—a half-hour later and the trick would have worked.

It was only when _____ sat bolt upright in his chair that I noticed he'd been slouching back at all, or that it was beginning to get too dark to see him clearly.

It took me a while to get to my feet. My legs were sore and stiff and I needed to put my cigarette out to have both my arms free to raise myself.

When I got so I could see out the window at what _____ was watching, it was a man in ripped trousers with his back to us, relieving himself on a pile of planks beside the stucco building's wall. He was hard to make out in the absence of street or window lights. When he was done, he hoisted his clothes around himself and picked up the least crushed of a pile of lightly spattered beer cans beside his right foot and drank from it.

He turned and walked in the direction of the building's entrance. Halfway there he stopped and vomited, emptying his head like a bucket. Then he went back inside the building, through the doorless entrance.

When I turned from the window, _____ was writing in his notebook, his hand curled around almost the whole pad, making an urgent script with movements so small he could have been shivering.

Once he had done, he checked his wristwatch, noted what I assumed was the time and then announced that we were leaving, that it was getting too dark to see.

The next day was the hottest since hell began. But we still got up and walked out into it, this time with more sandwiches and a couple of beers for _____. We walked with our jackets over our arms and the sweat made our hats and shirts sodden.

When we got to the imitation courthouse we'd been watching the day before, _____ circled round it, pressing himself into the wall and peering suspiciously through empty window frames at empty rooms, before we went and sat in the building across the road. _____ perched on the metal seat by the window, binoculars pressed into his face again. Again I sat on the ground.

I'd been using my hat to fan myself, and after we'd eaten the sandwiches it occurred to me to look for something that might make a better job of it, and I remembered the magazines in my coat pocket.

So I read back through Holcomb's story of the scientist who sent himself forward in time and also didn't. I read some of the story with the bloodthirsty alien tourists. Then I looked at the other magazine. It had on the front a submerged underwater craft of riveted red metal, with one big bulging window at its front. Swimming in the water through plants like streamers was a man with an air tank strapped to his back, carrying a harpoon. He was gesturing, alarmed, at the person inside the craft, who was green, ridged with fins, wore a gun on his hip and had two devil horns growing from the top of his head.

I read the story that went with that picture, though I don't know why I did it or what I was hoping for.

I read more and they weren't much better. _____ was taxidermy at the window and the magazine was junk. The room was hot and the floor was hard and tedious. I flicked pages, not fanning myself, not reading, doing nothing but flicking, until I realised that some words had jumped me on my way past, like fleas onto a passing dog. The words were 'the ball, copper and heavy-seeming' and they skipped and flipped about my head. They'd come from somewhere and it had to be the magazine. But I went looking for them and they'd gone, breezed.

Finally I cornered them, quivering at the top of a page under Holcomb's name. 'The ball, copper and heavy-seeming' they said. 'As to size, it was too large to hold comfortably in one hand.'

I read the story from the top. A man goes to sort the possessions of a friend—a brilliant friend, another genius, a scientist and a philosopher, who has gone bugs and been hauled out of his life, drooling and screaming, a hair-eating madman. And in sorting through the friend's filthy rags and torn-up books and stained bedsheets knotted in a noose, he finds this ball, the same one I'd seen sitting on Holcomb's desk. The same copper colour, the same size. I'd thought it was pitted with dots, but the story said it was scratched round by broken stripes in horizontal rings, and that squared with my memory and the story must have had it right.

As he goes about cleaning the remnants of his mad genius friend, the man puts his hand on the ball, and jumps back as if he's plugged himself into the lights. He's seen something, although he's not sure what. So he creeps up on the ball like it might scurry away, then he puts his hands around it and lifts it from its table. He's struck by images in crashing waves, and larger each time, and with them: sounds, too much, too everything, for him to make any sense of, and he has dropped the ball, and he is back inside the room.

He staggers, almost falls flat. Still he gathers himself together, and lifts the ball again. 'The great waves beat against him, their sound charged him, he felt as if he was being beaten by a fist as big as a man then big as a building then big as an island, but he held on even as around and above him patterns crawled like the constricting diamonds on the belly of a snake, that tightened its grip on the endless sky. He closed his eyes, thinking it might cost his mind to see, to try to make sense of the barrage.'

All the same he tries. He finds that he is standing 'in the cupped hands of a tremendous figure, who looked up and away, but was recognisably himself, and he saw above and past this giant imitation, to the same figure again and again, each so large that he held the last, and he, their original, gave a terrified shriek, and the cacophony of giants was so intense, he found himself back again in the room—where he had again dropped onto the table the copper ball.'

He starts looking through his friend's possessions differently, not arranging them for what to burn and what to keep, but looking for anything that might tell him what the ball is, and why it should be that he is driven mad with hallucinations when he touches it.

In the middle of an 'unremarkable black notebook' he finds a pencil sketch of the ball, complete with the scratched, dashed lines that ring it.

As he read the notebook he came to recognise in its scrawl and in the strange fiction it described both the friend he knew—the genius—and the lunatic he had clearly become.

It described the ball as containing everything, and as a device like a mirror reflecting the whole of the universe back to itself. His lost friend, or the madness that had possessed him, had written:

What I have made—what I have found that I have made—is a model of the universe perfect in every detail, in every component and every guiding principle, so it proceeds exactly in parallel with ours without ever diverging. To peer into it is to see exactly the instant of our own reality as it inevitably plays out, including your own peering into a mirroring reality of its own, like a man who finds himself under his own microscope.

Then, pages of frenzied script later:

I have somehow rotated it ever so slightly on a single axle, so that now it is slightly out of sync with our universe. The result, once you train yourself to adjust to its awful, fiery transport of sensation, is that you find yourself as if an actor standing on a proscenium, which contains within it another proscenium in which the actor who plays the part of you is, by the smallest moment, further into his performance than are you. And contained therein: another proscenium, another actor, further advanced, and so on, into the infinite. I have paused in my discovery to make this note, but my hand is shaking and I can barely breathe. To have sight to see what I now find it within my capacity to see: this is to intermingle with the divine.

The notebook contained much else after this febrile, barely comprehensible fantasying, page after page covered in looping ink, but not a single word that the reader could decipher.

Anyway, our friend reads this notebook and is all torn up about whether he can believe it: he is a sensible man but also a man who has seen something he can't otherwise explain. He sweats it out for a paragraph or two, then lifts the heavy globe again.

He was hurled back into the cacophony of giants. The firmament was filled, was *made* of the movement of familiar, monstrous bodies and he cowered in the great noise and endless waves of sight, and they cowered around and into him. He feared he would be crushed. He stood straight and in stages the sky widened around him, as each giant in turn, beginning with the one that seemed to hold him, stood straight. Very slowly he trained himself to focus only on one of the figures, three storeys above him. He raised an eyebrow, and maybe a dozen seconds later saw the same expression reach the face of this incomprehensibly large and distant him. He smiled and waited. And there: the smile, the length of a street, yet so human, so profound, and in his control, all of it was in his control. He felt a sensation of incredible strength at this army ringed around him in time and space. Above him with eyes glistening, there was a life as large as a sky, and above it another, larger still, and he could move them all as if puppets—it made him laugh. And the laugh became a crescendo through the bodies of the giants, that grew so loud it almost deafened him before it began to recede.

He put down the ball and found himself almost as unnerved to be covered by a roof as he had been to be swept away from it and deposited into the strange mirror, the universe of its own.

He reeled to the unmade bed and fell asleep dreaming of his own incredible strength.

When he woke he could hardly contain his desire to feel again that power, to be once more the animation at the centre of a universe. He went quickly to the ball, lifted it, and welcomed the violence of the giants' cacophony as it surrounded him. Feeling himself grown in confidence, he looked up into the infinite procession of his own body. It was fearful and incredible. A slight tremble of wonder at his own power took his hands, and the sky vibrated. He felt himself strung with the divine. Then a realisation seized him. There had been in the notebook a line: *like a man who finds himself under his own microscope*. For the first time, he looked, not *up* at the all-consuming vastness of the giants that surrounded him, but *down*, into his own hands.

There he saw a tiny figure he recognised as a miniature of himself. Around the figure was a small, round section of the world he thought he had left behind, as if suspended in an orb; the miniature peered down into its own hands, in which he made out another, smaller figure in a reality of its own which was also peering to a minuscule figure and world it held.

In an instant he realised the true meaning of his friend's creation. He might have thrilled to see the giants at his back enact his past, but these nesting dolls he held in his hands represented his true power. As they shrank into a point they were a lance that pierced the future.

Whatever he intended to do, he would see first begin to play out in his hands and he would know how he should proceed. Any misfortune would be avoided because he had become an entirely new type of creature: he had become a legion of infallible guides, guiding each other. The thought seemed to burn inside his head it was so large and intense: he felt barely capable of seeing to its farthest edges; it hurt him. He reassured himself with one section of the thought: he possessed a new, strange strength like nothing before it.

Then in his hands he was alarmed to see a movement climbing up the ladder of the tiny creatures towards him, closer and closer, they moved their heads as if in shock. It reached him: he gave the same motion. It was as if he were a string that had been plucked. Then he saw them lean in closer and in horror he followed them to see what drew their gaze.

He found himself hollowed: every capacity in him removed. In his confusion he was unsure whether he was himself or the creature he held: both, *all* froze in a dreadful paralysis. *Nothing*, he thought. *There is nothing I can do unless I see it performed first.* Madness swept towards him.

None of the creatures in his hand lay down the copper ball he had lifted when he thought himself free.

That was the story. Of all of it, the words that still turned in me were those first ones I saw, 'the ball, copper and heavy-seeming'. Whatever in Holcomb's story lit out from what was real, there was a straight tip somewhere deep in there. Because I had seen that ball sitting on his desk.

I put the magazine back into my pocket with the other two and walked around the empty box of a room. I stretched out my arm. The torn seam at the shoulder snarled at me. I sat back down on the ground beside _____, still pressing his eyes into his binoculars.

When I thought of the ball now, I could see it clearer than when it was sat in front of me. It was copper, it looked heavy, and it wasn't pitted with dots: it was ringed by broken lines.

The rest of the day died slowly. Nothing happened this time out, not that I saw and not that _____ saw through his little binoculars. Not even a bum slinking out to spray the wall.

The next morning, _____ and I walked back into the new

quarter, but we were only there through the morning. I reread the story with the copper ball and liked it more this time, knowing what would happen.

When I'd finished, _____ had already put away his binoculars, though they hadn't even dented his face yet, and it wasn't long before he was looking as often at his nails as out the window, or then at a coin he played with, turning it in his fingers and using it to bounce the light from the sun into his own eyes. Then he stood up, pushed his hat hard down on his head and stalked for the door, whistling for me to follow.

We went to the fairground, the first time in weeks, and rode the rides for a while. Then _____ folded a fin out of his pocket and gave it to the man by the target range and we shot pellets till even the toy guns got to feeling heavy.

After that we went to buy sandwiches and sweet, fizzing drinks from a stall at the rear of the park. We had to wait in line and then, when we were standing at the front, before a young mother tired from a day of having a horrible brat kid, _____ realised he didn't have any paper money left, and couldn't find any coins. My pockets were empty. The young mother started fuming, till _____ found a roll of pennies in his pocket he kept to use instead of knucks. He peeled open the roll and flicked the coins one by one across the counter and we sat and ate and drank.

We each ate half of a sandwich then we swapped, washing them down with the drinks. When I'd finished I asked _____ what we were going to do now. He said we were going to ride the rollercoaster and then he was going to go and pick up a woman and I could find someplace else to spend the night, and that's what we did.

There had only been a few nights since I had dragged my mattress to by _____'s bed that I'd slept anywhere else. There was the night on Holcomb's couch. Then there was one night I'd sat in Lydia's apartment, listening to her talk while she drank gin until she fell asleep, and I went walking about town, getting my feet wet in gutters and enjoying the emptiness of the streets.

I'd have gone to see Lydia, but the apartment manager still wasn't back and I didn't expect her to be in a mood to drink gin and tell jokes. Instead I went to a hotel, the New Europe, where I knew the house peeper on the night shift. In exchange for some company he would let me use one of the empty rooms, as long as I left it as I found it and I was gone before the end of his shift.

We sat in the radio room and listened to music. My peeper friend was in an armchair, looking like someone had just used him to mop up a spill and had only half wrung him out. He looked a lot shorter than he used to. We'd been in a bar once where he'd won a bet that he could lift me off the ground for ten seconds—I was allowed to fight it but not with my arms or legs. He'd struggled but he'd managed it, and there are plenty police wagons that wouldn't.

As some piano played through the radio he told me that

when he'd taken the night shift in the hotel he'd thought it might take him a while to adjust. He spent the first two weeks where every thought he had, there was always another thought behind it: he mimed playing the piano and said, 'Whatever was going on up here,' and he twirled the fingers on his right hand, 'down here,' and he did the same way over with the left, 'there was always this thought: I am earthly tired, yes sir.' And then after a couple of months he had realised that he had never stopped being tired—those chords were there, he had just stopped hearing them. It had been three years, and every day he was more tired.

A few hours later he was called to a room where there had been a disturbance. A drunk had thrown a bottle of scotch against his wall, irritating his neighbour, and then passed out, his breathing strained. I helped him carry the drunk across the street into an alley. We found a blanket behind an empty vegetable crate and laid it over him and went back to the radio room. If the drunk's breathing went from strained to stopped it wouldn't be good for my friend if it happened in the hotel.

My friend the house peeper sat back in his armchair, lighted his pipe and shook out the match. The piano music continued tinnily from behind the lit panel of the radio. He sighed with the grandness of a stately death.

'You hear that?' he asked, and his left hand played its keys in the air. Just then I couldn't hear anything else.

A while later I went and lay on top of the sheets in one of the unused rooms.

The next day I was to go back to babysitting Holcomb.

I knocked at his door, and the voice that came back was puny with fear. He was hiding behind his door frightened that a man had come knocking to kill him, and for a moment there was a thought that I could just take the part, and get it all done with, and I'd be doing the three of us a favour.

Instead I stayed in character as his babysitter, his faithful muscle, and he undid the three locks that were keeping him safe. He locked them all tight behind me, told me to take a seat, and went back to his typewriter. The copper ball was on his desk, on top of a stack of paper. As I went to my place on the couch, I felt as if I was edging around the ball, as if it filled the room, and when I was sitting it didn't matter where I tried to look, whether it was at Holcomb tapping away on his machine or the flies dying in his window, I'd immediately find myself looking at the ball again, like I was doing circuits round a phone booth or the inside of an ashtray.

Holcomb would sigh loudly to himself every once in a while, or light a cigarette, or look out the window as if some big sadness hung in the sky and he liked the way it lit him. I wanted to pick up the copper ball, or ask him about it, but the thought of either made me burn. I wanted to laugh at myself or boot my own teeth in—what a lug, what a dummy. I needed distraction.

I took the magazines from my pocket, but couldn't bring myself to read them. I put them down on a table in front of the couch beside a black notebook. I fed the brim of my hat through my fingers, round and round, until the spinning spread to my stomach and my head, and I started feeling ill.

Holcomb's tapping had picked up pace. I figured he wouldn't be paying me any notice and I took up the notebook. I read a page of it. It said,

We are crawling along the ground into a vicious headwind. Or, better, because we do not control the pace at which we move, we are being dragged. Though whatever is doing the dragging does not obstruct the wind, which is vicious and biting, and so intense that, as we are dragged through it we are reshaped by it, slowly, as a glacier bears through rock. As we are dragged forward, the buffeting of the wind elongates us. From small worms we are drawn out, our legs stretched, our chests, our pricks pulled long, we are lengthened finally to man height, and as the battering continues our skin is shaken by the wind, pulled from us until it is no longer taut, until it hangs and sags. And finally we are dragged through the vicious wind until our skin is torn from our skeleton, as the dragging continues, and awareness ceases, even if the dragging does not. We can cut the tether that pulls us forward, but we cannot turn off the wind. We can do nothing to escape the wind, but, in a limited way, we can free ourselves and explore ahead of the ever-forward dragging. We can send from our groove in the dirt emissaries of our

selves: though the ability is limited, it exists. These
emissaries

I went to turn the page when Holcomb's little kid hand
took the notebook away from me and returned it to the
table. 'You looking for words out of me, Box? There's a
fee.'

He sat down on the edge of the table, offered me a cigarette and lighted it for me. He looked at the magazines.
'Have you been reading these? "The Traveller in Time".
Look at this one.' He picked up the magazine with the fish-
man on the cover, his cigarette tucked tight in the corner
of his mouth. 'I can't remember what they called the story
in this one. I got a name stuck in my head for it, a terrible
name, "The Spherical Oracle", a dumb, terrible joke and
it got deep in my head and wouldn't leave, so I told them
to give it whatever name they'—he'd found the page and
his cigarette drooped in his mouth like he had just taken
one in the gut. '"The Spherical Oracle",' he read. 'Cripes.'

He flopped the magazines down.

I glanced over at the copper ball on the desk, and I
thought Holcomb's eyes narrowed, as if he had noted the
look.

He stood up and said, 'How about I make us some sandwiches?' and began pulling on his coat. 'Two blocks down
there's a sorry old bird who hasn't smiled since Gomorrah,
but he's got bread and cigarettes and he'll sell us them.'

He unlocked the door at length, then turned to me with

it open an inch. 'I thought you'd figured this thing out,' he said. 'Up! You stick with me.' I took my hat and made to get up.

And then howling rage came barrelling through the door, knocking Holcomb to the ground. He was bald, his sleeves were rolled short, and he bulged with anger: his head round his collar, his fists looking like they might burst through themselves they were squeezed so tight. He kept his howl up at Holcomb, who scrabbled back across the floor, and I got in between them, but he kept coming forward, a bald pulsing demon. 'I said I would kill you, so I came to kill you, Holcomb. This is what keeping a promise looks like, Holcomb'—and I knocked him in the chest and he howled at that too. He was old for a demon. He couldn't have been younger than fifty, and he was crying and he took a second to wipe at his tears with his fist, then he grabbed me round the middle, fixing my arms to my chest before I could stop him, and drove me back.

The desk crashed backwards with us.

There was a squeal in the room. It was Holcomb somewhere, begging me to help him, as if it was him that was being squeezed all out of life. I shook myself and this bald demon hung on and hung on but then hung on less and I got my breath back enough and knocked an elbow into his chest and then punched down onto his head, driving it into the edge of the desk. 'That little son of a bitch,' the crying demon said from the floor.

On the desk was the copper ball and I reached out for

it and I picked it up. It fitted in a single hand and I lifted it and as he raised up I crashed the ball into the side of his head, which crumpled with a sound like dropped fruit. He tried to wobble himself up and I hit him in the same spot. His ear caved in towards the strike like a car crashed off the road. I hit him again with the ball and left it in its fresh crater.

The man didn't move any more. The ball rolled out of the side of his head and under the couch, past Holcomb's feet.

Holcomb patted me on the back.

Interlude

Hector smiles at Charles, at the sourness of his expression. They have returned to their own compartment in the train. They are sitting. 'You're wanting to feel bad,' Hector says. 'You always want to feel bad.'

Charles has his feet raised on one of the padded benches. He has previously snarled at Hector and slapped him about the face and spat across his feet a bolt of saliva for saying things like this, but now he yawns.

'You're a dope,' says Hector, 'because you imagine you should feel bad, and you don't and it sours you. But why should you?'

'The buttons would make me feel bad for helping a man from the rear of a train,' says Charles.

'Sure, the buttons would like to make you feel bad,' says Hector. Hector presents Charles a cigarette without taking one for himself. Charles takes from his pocket an unremarkable matchbook and lights it. 'We understand how the police work,' Hector says. 'A dead body washes up at their desk. They say who did this? And they say why did they do this? And answers to questions like that are always easy. Every button you'll ever meet thinks he's got a great mind.' Charles gives a snort at this, it pushes two smoke plumes from his nostrils. Hector says, 'And the reason is they've never asked themselves a difficult question. You don't need a great mind to know that if you go in the rain without a hat your hair's going to get wet, and you don't need a great mind to know that if the wife's dead the husband killed her. The average button, if you were ever to give them a difficult question, they'd forget which way their knees bend.'

'So?' says Charles. 'Why did we throw him from the train?'

'Exactly what I mean,' says Hector. 'We could stay here and talk until you'd smoked me out of cigarettes and we'd still not have half an answer. There's no money to connect us to the man, and no grudge. The buttons can come and piece him together and ask the easy questions and they're not going to get an answer, and then they won't know what to do with themselves. Or else they'll go and find out that there's a wife, and she's wrapped around a boyfriend, and the whole thing looks good to them for an easy answer. However it happens, no police are ever going to knock on our door.'

'You're right,' says Charles. 'Society would disapprove of what we've done, but it's obvious why: for reasons of self-defence. If they don't know why violence has been visited on this person rather than that person, then they have to worry are their own necks safe.'

'Are their necks safe. Unreason and unpredictability are their own kinds of attack on society, which can only organise itself in response to the predictable. Without predictability, the best it can do is act randomly, and random actions are not a society at all. So in the face of aggression and unpredictability, in self-preservation, it would have to condemn us. However, it's absolutely clear that it will never have the opportunity: we will never be held to any account for what we have done.'

'Our own self-interest is not threatened,' says Charles, 'so the impulse that demands that society disapprove of our action doesn't lash at us. If we punish ourselves, then we are holding ourselves to a higher standard than that to which society holds itself.'

'And why,' says Hector, 'would it be reasonable to expect us to do that?'

'There's no question of feeling bad,' says Hector. 'And yet.'

'And yet,' says Charles.

'I'm unsure of how I do feel.'

'The experience is already being lost to a kind of vagueness.'

'I can remember the colour of his hair, something of his bearing,' says Hector.

'He didn't stand straight,' provides Charles, 'so although I had noticed he was tall, it was only as we grabbed him that I realised in fact quite how tall.'

'He lacked confidence and wanted to be left alone. He was annoyed when we interrupted his solitude, but he caught the expression of his annoyance quickly and made himself give a friendly smile.'

'His face was well creased from smiling. He had dark hair, beginning to fall to grey at the temples. He was dressed well but not expensively.'

'And I remember something of the cry he gave as he fell.'

'Yes, but that's all. Height, the colour of his hair, a kind of outline of a person, something of the cry,' says Charles. They sit in silence for some time. Hector has lighted a cigarette of his own and he looks down at its burning tip as though there is something to find there, or as if he might press it into his eye.

'Suppose,' says Hector, 'with the next one we go and sit with him. Perhaps they are in the dining car, and we strike up a conversation. We familiarise ourselves first. We get to know who he is, what he has by way of family, what sort of—'

'—God he believes in,' offers Charles. 'What sort of love he practises, what he thinks of—'

'—cities and cisterns. We take the time,' says Hector. 'We have the time. Then the whole experience might be more vivid, might endure more, sure, couldn't it? It'll last better when we throw him from the rear of the train or slit his throat or bash his head in.'

'It might,' says Charles. 'You're right about this one, after all. The yell still rings a bit in the mind, but faintly, and everything else has left.'

They move to the smoking car, and are aggrieved to find themselves its only inhabitants. To spend time, Charles asks Hector for the letter that has taken them on to the train journey, and rereads it. When he is done, Hector also rereads the letter, then returns it to his pocket. 'How do you know this woman?' asks Charles. 'Tell me as if I don't know.'

'I used to know her husband, the dead man,' says Hector. 'I went to his wedding, so I guess I met her there, but I don't remember her.'

The train pulls into a stop. Shortly after, a man joins them in the car, and Hector moves to sit beside Charles, so that together the two of them are opposite the new arrival. Hector lights the man's cigarette for him and they speak to him for some time. They learn a lot about his habits, and a lot of the details of his past, and commit a lot of his features to memory, but his yell as they throw him from the train still fails to compel itself on their minds.

PART 3

I took care of the demon's body while Holcomb hovered queasily, then I waited until dark and in two trips disposed of it.

I walked all the way back to _____'s. When I reached the apartment, there was a thought that I'd sooner see Lydia than _____, so I walked past our door and upstairs to hers.

There was still no apartment manager—she had taken over his work, collecting rent and complaints as needed, but she trailed around in it like a red-eyed ghost, and the smoke that drifted from her black cigarettes looked more substantial than she did.

She opened the door to me in her nightgown, and said, 'Hi, Box,' then fell back into her own bed in a way that suggested she would rather have been going out a window, or felt as if she was. I said hello back.

She looked smaller in her sadness, the way some animals lose size when they get wet. Still as death, eyes open, she lay shrunken in her sheets.

I took a seat on the ground by her bed. I thought to tell her that her husband would be back, and also wondered whether that would be a kindness, given it seemed unlikely that he would. I didn't say anything.

After a time, she patted me on the head, and said, 'Night, Box' and when I woke up I was still beside her bed.

I found _____ pulling on a tie. He said Jarecki had told him he didn't have to go back to the new quarter. He'd told him that we'd done good work.

I asked what we were going to do. _____ said we were going to go ask Jarecki for work. And if he didn't have any for us we were going to go knock over a bank, or ask Danskin if he had any, or play cards.

The club was open but it was early and the only business in the main room was a private bridge game in the corner. Through the office door I could hear _____'s raised voice.

A waitress took two brandies into the room on a tray. As she opened the door, more of _____'s shouting escaped like an angry wind let into a cold house. When she returned her tray was wet and held just one of the glasses, only now it was half the height and topped with a mountain range of glass. Her face didn't say much. I carried on waiting.

Bernard came up to me, his nose now entirely without bandages. He tapped it with a finger and winked at me. He was in a good mood—his face looked like a plate of meat in an advertisement painting, a hearty breakfast lit by a big orange sun. He explained that the lookout had told him we were around, and offered me a cigarette. I took it and we smoked silently.

Bernard asked if we were looking for work. I told him we were. He said that since Gabriel—who we'd spent those happy days bouncing off walls—had died, Fylan didn't have much choice but to keep some distance for a while, which was why there hadn't been anything for us.

My face must have asked a question, because he set to explaining.

Not long after we had returned Gabriel to Danskin he had puffed up with blood and died in a hospital bed. We were meant to deliver a beating, but a murder risked unbalancing things between Jarecki and Danskin.

No one blamed us for not knowing the boy was infirm, Bernard said, but in the spirit of caution, Fylan was keeping a space between Jarecki and the kid's death, and so also: us.

We finished our cigarettes. I got Bernard to tell me it again, just so I was clear with myself: we hadn't had any work from Fylan since we returned Gabriel.

He told me that's how it was, and how it would be, for a while longer, at least.

We'd been passed the envelope of cash, to keep us from wanting. Which meant the trips to the new quarter had been nothing, just _____'s invention. A play he'd put on so we'd have something to do.

The boy who'd come to our apartment with Bernard that first time—who'd stood flipping his knife open and shut—appeared. He whispered something to Bernard. Bernard told him, 'This is Box' and the boy nodded at me, and I nodded back. Bernard said they had to leave, but then he waved away the boy. He rubbed at the back of his neck with a hand. 'Look,' he said, quiet, 'I don't want you to feel sore I asked, but if you need to borrow some jack, until there's work again . . .' I thanked him, but told him I didn't. He nodded, patted me on the shoulder. 'As long as you don't feel sore I asked,' he said, and faded.

I didn't feel sore. I didn't feel too much about it at all, but the little I felt was like he had offered me a glass of water while I was being slowly buried: it was white of him but didn't enter into the problem. There was no work for us. We were going to be throwing cards, or sitting in empty buildings watching the sky. We weren't going to be able to take another breath, maybe not for weeks, and I needed air. I could imagine how the days would feel and it was like hanging on a clothesline, and my body ached with it already. But none of this was Bernard's fault.

I declined his offer decently enough I think.

When _____ came out it was in a cloud of anger. It drifted towards the exit and I followed after, but on the street I reached into it and pulled him out by the collar.

I had _____ off his feet and I shook him. I shook him for killing the boy and for leaving us with no work and for walking us into the new quarter to sit in dirt. I shook him but I didn't have any words for him, I just crackled nonsense and spat empty breath at him and he didn't kick, or shout or bite so nothing took, nothing started.

I set him back down. He said we'd go around the city, and we'd visit every person we'd ever done a favour for, and that's what we did.

No one had any work for us now. Not the pool hall prop, not the pawnshop owner, not the louse snow-peddler.

This was friendship in the city, this was fellow feeling. There was no one you could rely on when you needed a way to fill the days.

We took to throwing cards from a deck across the room and into _____'s hat, and we were at it still when the weekend came, and when it went.

The days were long. I slept as much as I could to shorten them. It was as far from enough as sleep is from death.

_____ shook me by the shoulder. I pretended to sleep through it. _____ left the apartment. I wanted to be asleep so badly but wanting it wasn't enough, it would have taken some improvement in me. Sleep was a capacity that other, better people had but I lacked. I went and cleaned myself. I threw water over my face and rubbed it dry with a towel, pressed more water into my eyes. I opened all the windows, standing by one to feel the chill, letting the rain come in and wet my bare feet.

Then I lay back down on the mattress and watched the ceiling. It had a couple of dark stains. Enough wrong with it to look a little interesting—malevolent, maybe—but it could only bear so much attention. I felt half bugs, like if

I stayed there I would have taken to chewing on the mattress, so I took a shower. Water hitting skin again, only now it made me itch. I sat in the kitchen, waiting for _____ to return. I had the feeling that I'd got sometimes when we had returned Gabriel and the work first dried up, the feeling that I was outside of the room looking in, and the room was empty. I looked at my arms on the table. They were folded and I had my hat in my hands.

I couldn't think of anything to do with my arms to make them appear more lifelike so I pushed my chair back and looked down at my shoes. I moved them to show there were feet inside and that the feet were mine, but I still felt like so much furniture. I decided that when _____ returned I would try and persuade him that we should fill our pockets with rocks and walk into the river. I doubted I would do it alone, but when we were together things got done.

For what felt like skin-crawling days I waited for _____.

When I woke up _____ was at the table with me and setting up for a poker game.

There were four players and two conversations, and I was sitting in the middle as if I was between two running streams. Holcomb had arrived—he kept his eyes away from me when he first came in—and now he sat talking to a salesman, someone I recognised from _____'s games without knowing his name. Meanwhile _____ was speaking intently to a man with one arm—the other, his right, just an empty sleeve pinned up beneath the shoulder—and one leg, the left, ending just below the knee and continuing in an aluminium pole. No one paid any attention to the cards or the small piles of chips on the table.

I couldn't make out either conversation over the noise of the other. It was _____ who was doing the talking on that side, all of it, while Holcomb was so tickled by whatever the salesman was telling him that he pulled his black notebook from his pocket and was asking questions, scribbling things down as he did.

The man _____ was talking at shuffled the deck. He was neat at it for having one arm. He dealt, and even though I'd been sitting it out, I took a card when he offered it, for something to do, and a while later, for more or less the same reason, when Holcomb poured me a drink from a bottle of gin I took that too.

After a while I'd begun to feel part of the game—the two conversations had turned into a communal, easy joking around, and I was up a few dollars. The only one of us down was the salesman, and Holcomb and _____ were riding him for it, and he was taking it with a sheepish good charm. The man with the one arm was called Childs. It was Holcomb that used the name: I still hadn't heard Childs himself say anything. I was thinking of asking him whether he was dumb as well as cripple. Either way I liked him for his quiet and I liked Holcomb's gin.

There was a big pot that ended with Holcomb and the salesman heads up, and the salesman lost again. After that he stood and said that, well, he'd had a good time, and he thanked us all for it, but the bank was going to have to close before it went out of business altogether.

He'd reached for his coat when Childs spoke. He said: 'Stay a while longer. I'll see you the cash.' The salesman looked surprised. I might have too if anyone was watching. Still, he gave his reason again, and added a couple more: he had to go and take a shower, he had an early train to catch.

He went for his coat again, and Childs stood, his chair scraping back from the table. Both the salesman and _____ reacted to the menace that had arrived to the cripple along with a voice. The salesman looked puzzled. Excitement swam and rippled in _____.

I couldn't guess if _____ had expected the scene to buckle, if there had been an agreement between him and Childs that it would, and I couldn't guess if he knew why it was important to Childs for the game to continue. More likely _____ was just a dog at the sight of a dinner bowl.

Childs told the salesman that he felt like playing some more, so he'd appreciate him sitting back down. 'I don't mean to put you out of pocket,' he said. 'I'll give you a sawbuck, if you win with it you pay it back, if you don't then you won't be in any debt to me.'

The salesman looked at Childs, weighing his thoughts. Either a man was offering him a friendly loan to keep a game of cards going, or else he was being taken hostage, and he was trying to figure which it was.

Maybe he thought the dimness of the room and the hanging smoke made the offer feel hostile. Maybe it was the look on _____'s face, which had a way of throwing a sinister cast on proceedings—his smirk like he was testing the edges of a person with the tip of a needle. Maybe the salesman thought that he obviously wasn't good at reading the table—he'd sat there and lost hand after hand after all—so he could be imagining a threat where none existed.

He tried to laugh, and then tried to put his coat on again.

Childs slapped the surface of the table and chips leapt from their stacks in alarm. His hand stayed on the table and along the back of his knuckles and folding around them ran a strip of metal. The salesman vibrated with the table top. Childs turned to me. He said, 'You a mute?'

I shook my head no.

He said, 'Get round the table and go through him, would you?' I went to the salesman, and patted him down. 'And the coat,' Childs said. Holcomb had his notebook out again, and was writing something down.

I peeled the coat from the salesman: there was a folding knife and an over-stuffed wallet in one of the pockets. 'Put them back in there and pass it,' said Childs and for no reason I can think of I did. He took the coat and walked it over to the hat-stand on his metal pole with its rubber hoof. He hung up the coat and then walked back to his space at the table and sat down. The salesman stuck hanging like a kite in a tree until Childs told him to sit down as well.

Childs slid the deck across the table to him, and then slid alongside it a pile of chips from his own stack. At some point, the strip of metal had gone from the back of Childs' hand, and again I'd missed the change.

He told the salesman to shuffle and deal. The salesman couldn't look at him, but he took the cards and he shuffled, and the game carried on, though quieter than it had before. A couple of hands later, pre-flop, the salesman started to shake. Then tears curled from his eyes and a mewling sound from his mouth. He started to ball up on himself, and Childs had to guide his cards upright so he kept them hidden. The game carried on while he wept.

I felt sore for the salesman, or bored now that the conversation had died in the game. Anyway, I heard myself say to Holcomb something about the machines in his stories—the ones that let you see into the future or communicate with the past. I said, 'What if you had something like that?'

He had been watching the crying salesman, and looked irritated that I was trying to speak to him. I asked him if he'd thought about what he might do with a machine like that.

'I've written stories about it. Of course I've thought about it,' he said, and that was it.

To keep myself from beating his face off his skull, I watched my cards.

With a machine I'd have gone back and kept myself from saying anything. I'd not have said anything but also I'd have known that the salesman was going to be kept in his chair by Childs and why. I'd have found out whether

_____ knew it was going to happen, and I would have kept myself on the same page as him. Instead the only thing I could think to do was ask this snot kid about his machine, because I didn't know what I was about. I was sick of being shrapnel, spinning out from something I had no say in.

I shouted something at the salesman to get him to stop his weeping, and when he didn't I cuffed him around the mouth, harder than I meant, and he started bleeding, until he was drooling blood towards his cards, for which _____ looked sore at me, which seemed to me an unkind response, seeing how little involved I'd been in making this scene. Anyway, I stood up and got a towel and threw it to the salesman to hold to his cut. And we sat there, playing cards in silence with a weeping, bleeding man until Swagger walked in.

We heard his footsteps so clear—all the way from the front door of the apartment building—that they sounded made for the radio. When he opened the door I noticed that we'd all been watching in anticipation, staring at the entrance as if we were at the greatest leg show on earth: no one had said a word, mid-hand we'd forgotten the cards. The salesman had stopped mewling, probably hadn't even remembered to bleed.

Swagger opened the door to _____'s apartment and took it in like it was a well-remembered part of a vast kingdom. He gave a nod to Childs, and hung his hat. He stood almost as tall as me and his jacket was well made, so it left barely a hint of the big revolver that sat in his shoulder rig. The salesman started up crying again.

Swagger walked to the table, saying, 'I hope you don't mind me intruding on your game.' He flashed a Photostat licence that said:

Mike Swagger.

He was shamus, not cop. 'I've got a few questions I'd like to ask Polk here about why he's in my town, and a few notions I'd like to put in his head about the importance of learning lessons and appreciating good luck.'

Childs had carried his chair over to beside the salesman—Polk—and now Swagger sat. He pulled the towel away from Polk's face to look at the wound, and then up at Childs. Childs gave an almost invisible nod in my direction, and Swagger sized me up. He gave what felt like a look of appreciation, and said to the salesman, 'Looks like that could have been a deal worse. In all else neither the long or the short of it looks good for you, Polk.'

Polk sniffled angrily. He was still holding his cards as if the game might start up again at any second, and it was them he spoke to. 'I think I told you everything I had to say already today, Detective Swagger. I was helpful, I was accommodating, but if it's thanks to you I've been kept here'—he gestured angrily at Childs, his voice growing loud and piercing, like an insect almost buzzing into your ear—'and I've been beaten'—then at me, and his face and neck bloomed with colour like he was being dipped in ink—'then I'm going to find that policeman, that Cromarty, and I'm going to report this harassment.'

'When you were good enough to talk to me earlier, Polk,' said Swagger, 'you made clear you knew nothing about a sordid little gang, a club of photography enthusiasts, that I was trying to locate a member of—the queen of the place. This gang have something like a membership badge, or a key.' He slid one of the playing cards along the table, and tore it along its length, pinning one corner so he could make a neat jagged rip through it. He held the two halves up separately at shoulder width. 'This private club holds a deck of half cards,' he said, 'and every member comes along, and has their own half card.' Swagger put the two halves together and showed how neatly they fit. Polk sweated.

Swagger took something from his pocket and put it flat on the table under his hand. 'You were smart enough not to keep it on your person, but you couldn't bring yourself to get rid of it could you, Polk? You figured you'd skip town a short while and when you came back, you'd go back to your little club, and enjoy some more of your games.' He lifted his hand. Underneath it was half of a queen of diamonds. She had been cut longways down the middle, between the eyes, leaving a serrated, knife-cut edge. 'I'm afraid, Polk,' Swagger said, 'I'm cancelling the trip you're all packed for. Instead we're going to see Cromarty, and I bet he'll have his own thoughts on where you'll take your vacation.'

Polk gulped like he was swallowing a bad year. 'Detective Swagger,' he said, and his voice was almost calm. 'Swagger, I know I've made mistakes.'

Swagger shook his head. 'Typists make mistakes, Polk. A girl's dead—two if you count the child she was carrying. That's not a mistake. What do you figure the odds are that child was yours?'

'Swagger,' said Polk, 'I know it's bad, and if I had nothing to offer I'd have nothing to say. But I've got something to offer and you want to hear it.'

Swagger put the cut card back in his pocket, 'You think you can buy me, Polk?' he said.

'Swagger, look, if I didn't have anything to sell, I'd have nothing to say, but I've got something to sell, and we need to go somewhere to talk about it.' He gestured at us, at their audience.

Swagger yawned unhurriedly, then said, 'I gave you a chance to talk, Polk, and you fed me a line. I spent half of today chasing down what you sold me, and it was a rotten bill of goods. About as rotten as I've ever seen.' He slammed his big hands down flat on the table. 'But, we do have to go. You can talk all you want on the way, Polk, but I'm weary from listening.'

Childs had taken up position beside Polk's chair. Now he took him by the arm. Polk stood but then shook off Childs and began to make another complaint. Childs clapped him on the back of the head and drove him forward, only letting him gather his hat and his coat, then driving him on again, like an uncooperative rock he was kicking along the street.

Swagger walked to the threshold, collected his own coat, and faced us while he pulled it on. With his hat held decently at his chest, like a man passing on condolences, he said, 'I'm sorry to have interrupted the game,' and left.

As soon as they'd gone, there began a feeling of a missed opportunity. It felt as if I'd eaten well in a dream and woken hungry. But before the feeling had much of a chance to take hold, Holcomb upped and out of the room after Swagger. That left me and _____ and fifty-one cards that hadn't been torn in half.

_____ poured the money Polk, Childs and Holcomb had left into his pocket, tipped us each a drink from Holcomb's bottle and took his over to the couch, where he slugged it back and lay down with his eyes shut.

I went to the window and saw Holcomb and the big detective in conversation at the corner of the building, while Childs kept hold of Polk nearby. I wondered why Polk didn't break free from the cripple, and wondered what Swagger and Holcomb were talking about, and finished the drink and went and poured myself another, and then a third. I was happy that it made me feel like a ball on a downhill slope—I've never much drunk, but found myself wanting it now. If a feeling like that could become something you want then maybe all things could, and Polk could be happy waiting for Swagger and Childs to escort him off to whatever justice they had ready for him, and Lydia could like sinking into her sorrow and her sheets until there was nothing left of her but a stain, and I could get to enjoy seeing lips flapping on street corners and not need an idea of what was being said, and just pour myself another slug of gin. I spun downhill a bit further and in the bedroom I lay down on _____'s bed and slept.

A day or a week later, and no work in between, _____ and I went to a bar—a second-floor dive without much in the way of either comfort or custom. _____ bought a pint of bourbon and drank it with a grim determination. I drank water and chewed on my tongue and counted and recounted the number of noses on each face around me and never got a surprise.

_____ got into conversation with three young men. They must have been brothers. Each of them was scrawny and red haired and they spoke in a vicious whisper that seemed to come out of all three of them at the same time. After a while _____ called me over and introduced me and told me that they had a plan for us to earn some money. I shook hands with the three of them in turn or with one of them three times, their hands slipping in and out of my grip, and they explained in their shared harsh whisper their plan. _____ and I would be two strangers out in the world. We would get into a fight. Once we had a big enough crowd interested in us, the three red-haired brothers would go through the pockets of our distracted audience. Afterwards, we'd come back to the second-floor dive and split the money.

It was the sort of scam _____ often didn't have any time for, but it looked better than boredom. _____ agreed for us. For a while the triplets whispered at each other about where we could find the best crowd. They settled on a tourist hangout in the centre of town.

They wanted to stay and work some more on the pint of bourbon, but _____ was keen to get started, so he pushed the cork in the bottle and the bottle into his jacket and was out the door with his hat on his head while they were still holding their glasses out to his seat.

We took the streetcar out near a big theatre that brought in the crowds in droves. Unfortunately, it already had for the evening: the show had started and they were inside, out of reach. The most business we could find was outside a hotel, where hacks stopped to collect rich tourists and a couple of newspaper stands had a few customers flicking through the evening edition. The triplets thought we should go and share the bourbon, wait for things to pick up and come back when the show closed, but _____ wasn't in a mood to wait. He told me to go and stand on the other side of the street.

I went over to the bigger newsstand. A gent taking his pipe out for a walk gave me a sidelong glance, twitched the pipe with alarm, then remembered an appointment he had not to be around. However it was I looked, apparently it wasn't casual. The stallkeeper asked me if I was looking for something. I tried having my hands in my pockets but it didn't feel right. Then _____ had managed to fall over my legs and was accusing me of tripping him.

It might have made a better show if I had tried to reason with him, but I know what _____'s like, so instead of wasting time I took a swing at him with my right. _____ was quick and managed to dodge it, then as I was beginning to throw out my other arm, he got in under it and lifted his knee into my side. He was trying to hit me above the hip, where it might have hurt me, but I was too tall for it. Once he'd done I swiped him with the back of my left hand. It brought colour into his cheek and I would have given him a line about his pretty blushes, but I wouldn't have got the words in time and anyway he popped me in the jaw so hard it nearly took the floor out from under me.

That cinched the notion that I didn't want _____ hitting me any more.

I grabbed his jacket back and off his shoulder with one hand so he staggered and the jacket would hinder his arms, and tried to put the boot into the back of his legs and knock at his neck or his face to get him on the ground. He went down on one knee, but he had his arm up to block the punch to his neck. And he pushed himself forward, throwing his weight into my legs and pinning them together.

As my head hit the sidewalk I thought I saw a policeman through the legs of the gathering crowd, walking off with a smile on his face. That was the sort of casual I had wanted to be—the casual of a button walking away from a brawl in the street. Then _____ fell on me with fists and a sharp knee.

The racket was that we would be pulled apart—the decent onlookers of our good city would intervene and the intervention would be a part of the spectacle we created while the bleak triplets worked their way through the crowd. But we were going at it too good for anyone to want to step in.

As _____ started to beat my face, I was aware of the crowd swaying. People at the back grew keen to see what was happening while the people who could see didn't want to get too close to it.

It seemed a better idea, from a particular point of view, that I slug _____ until he passed out than that he slugged me until I passed out. Apart from anything else, I would in all likelihood lay off _____ once he was out and I couldn't be completely sure of the same courtesy from him. So I managed to throw him away from me and had just caught him with one fairly good fist above his right eye when he was being pulled backwards.

The figure holding his left arm said to me, 'Woah.' The same figure holding his right, said, 'Patty. Lay off.'

I took a couple more small steps in their direction, trying to keep the ground from squirming out from under me. The crowd swayed more, and so did the sky and the faces of the matching pair on either side of _____. Dogs looked on but they didn't bark.

I found my feet. No one was trying to hold me back. _____ wasn't fighting against the two red ghouls holding him. I thought there was maybe blood on my face but I put my hand on it and as far as I could tell it was just sweat. My eye hurt. I turned around and walked away.

Somehow the four of them made it back to the second-floor dive bar before me. Maybe it was the limp that had started after a block or two, or that I got a bit lost after the headache began in earnest.

They had wallets and money clips spread out on the table in front of them. _____ looked happier than he'd looked in a week. His lip was split open on one side. His forehead had a pretty good lump on it. I drank a glass of water and stopped thinking about my head and shards of glass and vicious teeth. It didn't help.

The triplets weren't in as good a mood as _____. They were complaining to him about the haul, saying they would have made more if we'd waited, and that the fight had been too much. The same mouth made each complaint three times from different seats. They complained that they had to separate us, so we'd all been seen together. _____ shouted at them that what did they care. You couldn't have picked one of them out of a line-up that only had the three of them in it, he said angrily, but he couldn't stop grinning.

They whined some more, hoping for a bigger cut of the money. Whether _____ figured that was what they were hoping for I didn't know. I was sure they'd already taken one anyway.

The barman brought over another pint of bourbon and _____ paid him from one of the clips on the table. He took the money like it was innocent as milk from the breast.

When the joint closed all five of us landed up back in the apartment. Immediately _____ collapsed in his bed, but for what felt like an age I had to play a tiring game: one of the three pickpockets was sprawled over my mattress and I had to lift him by the scruff of the neck and the back of his belt and put him out the way in a corner of the room. Except, when I came back another one was in the same place, and I had to grab him and clear him out my way. And then the same with the third one, or with one of the first two all over again.

When I finally got down on the mattress I thought my dreams would be full of scrawny redheaded pickpockets I'd keep having to move and re-move, filling closets with them, building dams, finding them among the pipes beneath sinks and hidden in hollow curtain rails, and sewn into the back of chairs. But if I had any dreams no one was writing them down.

Bernard came to the door, with his knife-flipping boy. He told us that we had some work from Jarecki, and _____ almost danced on the spot. I could almost have joined him.

It was more debt collection. This time the debt belonged

to Holcomb, and it was enough money that unless he'd inherited a movie studio or an oil well we didn't know about, it didn't seem likely he'd be able to pay.

That didn't matter to us. _____ beamed at getting work, but it was nothing to how I felt. I was heated by gratitude, sweating with it. I may have patted Bernard on the back as he left, I was so excited, like a big child, like _____ on his way to a rollercoaster.

It was more than just work. It was a winning ticket, a chance to undo the conversation: the question I'd asked Holcomb about his machines and the humiliating, spiteful little non-answer he'd given me. We'd go and speak to Holcomb, and this time he'd want to speak to us. He'd turn on that mouth of his, set it running, and talk to us about anything we wanted him to talk about. Because he'd be scared. And if he didn't, we could take a toe or cut off an ear, as we liked, until he offered some proper information.

By the time we crept up to the end of the line, it was dark. The lights of a phone booth and the streetlights above appeared to us out of the rain, like a boxy moon and past-ripe stars.

The rain was keeping the street clear of people, although we had to walk around two kids who were holding down a third, silent and unmoving, slapping him across the face and the belly while their short-sleeved shirts soaked through. Playing at policemen, maybe. A large man on the other side of the street lowered his hat against the weather as he passed us, then was gone around a corner.

We made our way to the second floor: _____ was about to start kicking at doors and threatening households in neat order, but I had been here before, and told him so. He didn't seem to care. I knocked at Holcomb's door and it swung open without complaint. There was no answer as _____ announced us.

The typewriter was undressed, its dark, tank-like case on the ground. On the desk sloped, shameful, a pile of magazines. _____ threw one to me. It was a love pulp. Sure enough, Holcomb's name was inside, though it came cross-dressed, with a new feminine forename. I dropped it back into place. I looked around for the copper ball, but it was gone. Then _____ gave a long, low whistle of appreciation. He had opened the door through to the bedroom and stood looking in. I walked over.

The house edge had got to Holcomb.

He lay on his front on the bed, his head tilted up, his chin propped on the mattress so that he looked directly at us. He looked like he had taken a beating, and that it wasn't the only bad thing to happen to him recently. _____ lighted a cigarette and we went into the room. One of Holcomb's eyes was swollen and purple. It bulged out from his face like a piece of fruit ready to drop off a bush. There was a dark patch in his light hair.

When we turned him over we found a neck you could have ridden a streetcar over for all the difference it would make, a neck spun into a rat tail. In his mouth he still had a few teeth. And in his left cheek, just above the line of his stubble he had the small round hole of a .32—a little mouth, caught in a surprised little 'o'.

_____ ran his little finger around the rim of the hole. He said, 'Where do you suppose he keeps his money?'

We looked. We checked under pillows, in pockets, behind drawers, under loose floorboards and in any likely looking books. I patted Holcomb down and pulled off his shoes. We didn't find anything. We didn't know if there was anything to find.

Outside the street was deserted. Maybe the city's always so still just before shots are fired. Certainly no one's ever known to see anything they didn't want to see.

We sheltered a moment in the lobby. Rain was streaking past the only lights—the streetlights and expressionless windows—and noisily hitting the street. As we stepped forward I saw a mass of something lying on the ground at the dark phone booth. It hadn't been there before.

I bent down and picked up a heavy rock the size of a deck of playing cards, there for a doorstop. _____ hadn't seen the shape by the phone booth. He started to snarl at me for blocking his way. I knocked him over the threshold back into the building, then turned and heaved the rock toward the mass, and kept turning, throwing my own weight through the street door. Before I hit the cool lobby floor there was a shot, the sound of the bullet hammering into the doorframe, another, and a shattering as the rock

I'd thrown found the glass of the phone booth.

As he got his legs out from under me, _____ kicked me irritably in the jaw. On the street there was nothing left to see. The mass on the ground was gone. The door on the phone booth swung jerkily shut and, as it closed, the light inside flickered on. Apart from some broken glass and two bullets in a doorframe instead of in some dumb muscle, all was as it was meant to be. The rain kept falling.

I was glad to have kept from getting shot. But Holcomb was dead, and I'd needed to talk to him. I'd have made him say what he knew about how we move through time. I would have made him say what was just stories and what he knew beyond what he could fit into pulp magazines. Because Holcomb knew something. I knew by now, was certain: from a living Holcomb I could have learned how to take time and shake second chances from it. Now he was dead and everything was more set and certain.

It would have been good to go and sleep, but some movement was unavoidable: we had to go and tell Fylan that he'd sent us to get money from a corpse.

Bernard commiserated with me, about the trouble we'd had, about the writer's corpse lying in the bed and ours meant for the gutter, but he explained this about debt. He said that on the other side of the office door, Fylan wasn't going to be impressed with any explanations that _____ might be giving in there. 'You should have brought back his fillings—something,' he said. I nodded, though if the writer had any fillings they'd already gone out the door or down the back of his throat.

That night _____ was sore from being shouted at and sore from being shot at, and the next day we went looking for Holcomb's girl, because it was Holcomb's girl Fylan had bestowed the debt on. After you die all the people you know would sooner put a match to all the things that matter to you than have to sign a receipt. Lawyers and landlords won't search hard for a home for your fondest memories. The one thing that always gets inherited is debt. When your life hits that dead end, know that your debt keeps moving. And we were sent running after it.

We'd never known anything about a girl when he was alive, and the apartment where Holcomb had stopped bleeding for the last time hadn't hinted at her presence. But it didn't matter: the debt was hers now. Just like the shoes on my feet were mine and the streets belonged to whoever rode along them most expensively.

We had two addresses for her—her apartment and the dentist where she worked as an assistant. It's easier to embarrass people at their work and smarter to hurt them at their home, so our first call was to the dentist.

The dentist was called Boken. His business was pristine. The anteroom shone, from the floors to the receptionist, while around it the building fell apart and the neighbourhood rotted. It was a birdhouse painted baby blue and set in a dead tree.

An old man perched on the edge of his chair and a young woman clutched the bag in her lap. The receptionist in spotless medical whites eyed us cautiously from behind a counter and the inch-thick glass of her spectacles. She sat in a booth of diagrams of bisected molars and slogans about flossing, and twice-life-sized replicas of beautiful teeth. There was a price list above her shoulder and she was tapping a pen against an appointment book that lay open in front of her.

_____ lighted a cigarette and approached. He asked her civilly whether she was Evelyn Heydt. She told him no and asked if he'd take a seat. He told her no and smiled at her. She looked unnerved. Her eyes moved to his teeth. Professional interest maybe. She backed from her booth, slipping through a door in the rear. 'Keep the sun in your smile!' said one of the posters.

_____ sat by the girl, sunning her with his smile. She clutched her bag a notch tighter. He asked her if they knew each other, and mentioned the name of the madam who considered him a guardian of young love. She kept her eyes on the glistening floor tiles.

The old man pushed himself up on an old wooden stick the colour of tar and started shouting he wasn't going to be kept waiting while one more someone else without an appointment went to see Boken before him.

If they were going to do much of anything for the old man they were going to have to find his teeth first. He asked us if we knew what piles were, and said that he would tell us exactly what they were. 'Little balloons of blood, right across the verge of your rectum—imagine that, you rotten damn pair,' he said. He asked us what we thought sitting on a waiting room chair with piles felt like, and then promised to tell us exactly what it felt like.

Conventional wisdom held that the sadness in the girl's eyes would have been more moving if she was beautiful. _____ frowned, maybe thinking about piles, maybe not. The pile sufferer suffered.

When the receptionist returned she moved her appointment book to the side and lifted up a hinged section of the counter, then she asked if the two gentlemen would come through, which we took to be us. As we passed, she pressed herself into the wall like she was pushing herself through a grille. No one listened to the complaints of the old man sitting on his balloons of blood.

A man in a white smock opened the door at the end of the short hall as we reached it. He looked at us, then told us we weren't police in a way that suggested the waiter had brought the wrong kind of soup at an inappropriate temperature. I walked him backwards into the room.

It was cramped and immaculate. No child ever had a better-dusted dollhouse. The underside of a bed made up part of a wall, but to fold it down, you'd have had to move the white chair with boughs of lights, mirrors and lenses that filled the middle of the room. And to move the chair you'd have to move the detective, Swagger, who was sitting in it, wearing the grin of a sportsman the official hasn't spotted standing on someone's neck. In the corner of the room, filed away like an instrument on a tray, standing on one leather shoe and one rubber hoof, was Childs.

'No, they're not police, are you, boys?' Swagger said. As he spoke he crossed his raised legs, placed his hat on his chest and folded his arms behind his head.

Childs stepped forward and gestured for us to lift our arms so he could fan us. _____ bristled and snarled, but before anything could happen Swagger cut in. 'Leave that out, Childs,' he said. 'We're not here to knock heads or get in anyone's way. In fact, I'd bet we're here for exactly the same reason as these boys are.' He made his big face into a question mark a mile high and directed it at _____.

_____ didn't respond. He'd sunk into a brewing anger the moment Childs moved to go through him. Now Swagger might as well have been a car taking too long at the lights. _____ waited and then he told the room that we hadn't come to have our teeth picked but to find out where Evelyn Heydt was, and that a dick licence and a cripple weren't enough to keep us from asking what we'd come to ask. I was watching Swagger in his dentist's chair and I saw his smile disappear before he had time to fix it back on. But when he did, Swagger just clapped his hands together like cymbals. 'I knew it!' he said. 'We've just been asking the same thing. Our friend Mr Boken here doesn't have too strong a fix on that.' He looked at Boken to elaborate.

Boken said that she should have been in for work two hours ago but hadn't arrived. 'Mr Boken,' Swagger said, 'says it's not like her not to come in—in fact it's never happened before. Isn't that right, Mr Boken?' Boken nodded. Boken had started to sweat: he took a sharply folded white handkerchief from a pocket and dabbed at his wet top lip with it.

_____ looked at Swagger, then at the dentist, then he turned on his heel and we started to walk out the room.

'Let me buy you boys a drink,' the big shamus said behind us. We kept walking.

Even as we walked out of the reception he was behind us. 'Let me buy you boys a drink,' he said. 'Don't you want a chance to talk?'

We'd reached the home of Evelyn Heydt when _____ put his hand across my chest and stopped me where I was. I followed his gaze up to a window of the building. There was a girl framed there, backlit and beautiful, brushing her hair. A dagger-thin split between her blood-red lips, her hair following in brown folds down onto her shoulders and slipping like fingers onto the straps of her dress.

We'd hustled to get there like we were being tugged along on a string, but now we stopped and watched while Evelyn Heydt—because who else could it be?—finished brushing every lock of her hair, and who knows how long it took. Finally she laid down her brush, walked to the window like a movie star accepting an award and lowered the curtain on the whole scene, and right then, dead on cue, out from the wings a delivery boy: a kid escorting a stack of groceries almost his size. We intercepted him at the door. _____ reassured the kid that Miss Heydt would get her groceries—they were hers of course—and that besides he'd have other things to worry about if he didn't beat it. I felt bad about it, if only because you could see from the kid's face that delivering groceries to Evelyn Heydt was the best thing his weeks had to offer.

I carried the groceries, and _____ knocked sharp on her door and covered the peephole with his palm. A voice, unclouded and bright as a summer day in better places: 'Who is it?'

_____ said it was her groceries and she opened up.

A flood of desire came at us through the door, this charged moment of seeing the beautiful face from the window again, but now also the dress, and the quieted, deafening body beneath it. But something else must have pushed back in the other direction from us. She stepped away like she was chased and we had to move after her, we were after it now—we were pulled forward, we were awake.

_____ laid the delivery crate down on a chair and took a quart of gin from it and cracked that open. The apartment smelled like Evelyn Heydt, her deep driven scent. She stood scared in this rich beautiful space that was completely hers, standing as straight and unnatural as a nail that had just been pounded into it. Her eyes big as spot-lights. Her lips fell redly apart. 'Who are you?' she said. 'What do you want?'

_____ finished drinking from the gin and laid it down, and he took his little butterfly knife from his pocket and slowly unfolded it. As Evelyn Heydt was retreating into herself, diminishing into a small and solitary part of the room, we were expanding, growing out, it was our stage now and it was beginning to feel good to stand on it, and have her eyes on us, fearful, quivering. _____ took his knife and I thought about taking some rope, or a sheet. We could blindfold her and carry her out, bundle her into the boot of a car, or we could keep her here until she understood exactly what was required of her. But first we stalked her across the room, and again she asked us what we wanted. Every angle and curve from the nape of her neck to her calves and her ankles formed like a letter in a perfect sentence on the surface of my tongue, my mouth full of words. _____ swung his knife lazily before himself, and said, 'Why don't you tell her what we came for, Box.'

She was into the window, her legs bending as her hips pressed back onto the sill, her back pressing against the glass. My mouth turned over the new sibilant curves in the new folds of her dress, the coiled vowels of distress behind her mouth. Now, it was now: I opened my mouth. 'Holcomb's dead,' I told her, 'and you're—'

—and then _____ was struck and _____ struck the ground. I started to turn but a knock to the back of my neck and another to my legs, and I was on one knee, and there was a small metallic snicker. Trying to move forward tipped me painfully sideways. My left wrist was hand-cuffed to my right ankle.

With my cheek against the carpet I saw Mike Swagger, private detective, stagily kick _____'s knife away across the room, and his feet sidle around us. The love interest flung her arms around him, 'Oh thank God, Mike, thank God you made it here just in time!'

It was a tough scene to watch.

'Don't worry kid, but let's get out of here,' said the shamus. 'You two so much as wag your tails too hard and there's lead coming back through this door for you to fetch.' And then with the love interest pressed behind him, he circled us, his gun carefully fixing the unconscious _____ and the immobile me, and they made their exit.

I tried to move and the same pain that had tipped me on my side dug into me, so I stopped trying. I didn't want to wait too long for _____ to come round so I used my free hand to slap and shake his face. Eventually his eyes opened and simultaneously he spat at me, a thin rope of spit that slicked across my eye and cheek. Once he was awake, he went to the dressing table and recovered his lit-tle knife from under it. He took a couple of hairpins from a drawer, and used them to relieve me of my cuffs. I wiped away his spit, which hung like spun sugar about my eye-lashes.

It didn't bear to stick around, not when the cops seemed bound to be on their way, expecting to find us trussed and waiting. So we blew.

But outside, standing beneath a tree on his rubber hoof, taking the air, was Childs, Swagger's gunsel.

The smart play would have been to spin on our heels and head off in the other direction, until we'd put enough distance between ourselves and the place of certain recent threatening behaviour, until everything started looking a bit hazier and more subjective. This was the sound legal counsel. But we were bruised and sore and it seemed like a pleasure to give Swagger the straight goods on whether a cripple was enough to hold us tight, so we headed straight for Childs.

_____ snarled at him a little and pulled out the butterfly knife again. He said, 'Tell your elbow that the next time I'll see him coming, and when I do I'm going to knock his beak through the roof of his hat.'

Childs didn't step back from the knife, or pull out his brass knuckles, but he looked over his shoulder, with its empty flap of sleeve, and there was Swagger, walking toward us, closer than hell, close as sweat to skin, and _____ reared like a startled horse but then widened his shoulders and seemed ready to jump on the detective, to clamber up him, like a man swinging his way up the side of a building to punch through the windows.

Swagger held up big peaceful paws. 'Look,' he said, 'that

scene up there was no damn good. And I hope you boys know I realise that. But we're none of us green. We all know how the game is played. And I tried to make the set-up clear, to sit down and talk you into this situation properly before you marched over here. You wouldn't hear it then.'

The detective paused. _____ still bristled, but Swagger was at his ease. There was nothing defensive in the way he held up one hand as he spoke. There was no sign that he was expecting a lunge from _____, which was something you wanted to be ready for if it was coming.

'I want things to be jake between us,' Swagger said. 'I can appreciate good workmanship wherever I see it, and the way you were putting the fright into that frail up there, that was something special. You do good work: I knew that the moment I saw you, back when I had to lift Polk out of your card game, and I'm not going to make it my business to hurt your business.'

By now _____ was looking at the gumshoe with something more like curiosity than spite. His butterfly knife hung limp like a spoon in the hand of a kid who's finished a sundae.

'Listen,' said Swagger, 'the last thing I want to do is get in a position where I have to go toe-to-toe with a couple of tough loogans such as yourselves. I got through it once, by the skin of my teeth's skin, but that doesn't make me keen to go up against you again. So how about we go and I buy us all a drink and we can have a talk and I can set things jake between us?'

Once, back when he had a working neck, a lot more teeth and one less hole in his head, I'd watched Holcomb on a bad streak at a poker game, losing money at each hand and just tilting harder after it on the next. When he'd lost all he had to lose and as much as the rest of the table was willing to take from him in promises, he'd sat back in his chair with a smile on his face that said that if nothing else he was at least drunk. Then he started talking about 'people', which was how he often talked about himself, and about how they'd sometimes get the feeling that they didn't know why they made the decisions they made or acted the way they acted: like the real business of everything being felt by them was actually being conducted somewhere far away.

I thought that made some sense, that it was a notion people probably got a lot more than they admitted.

At any rate, we agreed to the drink.

'There's not many,' said Swagger, 'could ask for a glass of water in this place and walk out intact.' He laughed and clapped me hard across the shoulders. We made for a table. The man sitting at it had memorable ears, ears like a mudslide: I'd seen him box once. When he saw the big shamus carrying a mess of drinks toward him he cleared out, wiping his seat down with his cap before he left. He had somewhere else to be. We took our seats and Swagger pushed a whisky into _____'s hand, and raised his own in a toast. 'To bygones!' he said and knocked it back. _____

sipped suspiciously. The cripple and I watched.

'I meant every word I said back there, boys, I hope you know that. Damn fine work. And I don't begrudge you putting the scare on Evelyn Heydt, and I hope you don't begrudge me doing my job either.' He took a gulp of beer and wiped the foam from his lip with the cuff of his shirt. I drank some of my water. Without taking his wary eyes off Swagger, _____ had finished his whisky and started on a beer.

If _____ had ever cared what had brought Swagger to Evelyn Heydt's door then by the time he was four drinks in the curiosity had left him. He seemed content to drink and listen to Swagger's stories. Swagger had moved from telling us how much he hoped we understood to talking about the war. Swagger had seen things in the war.

'I once saw a man dying on the ground, his wife—his goddamned beautiful young wife—and his three young kids gathered round him weeping, the ground muddy and red from his blood and their tears. It was goddamned tragic,' Swagger said. 'Enough to make a weak man cry. I'd shot him. You got to do things like that in the war, and no one asking to see a licence or taking statements about whether their back was turned or if they were armed. Tragic, of course, but necessary. I blew a hole in his chest the kids could have crawled up in. Childs was there.' He gestured to the cripple who was turning his finger round the rim of his glass of beer and watching Swagger talk. We were all watching him talk, but not, you got the idea, the same way Childs was. 'He took a bullet for me that day. Caught it beneath the shoulder. It cost him that arm. The only friend I've ever had worth a damn, and the only man I'd trust when the lead's set to fly. He saved my life when he caught that bullet. I got my revenge though. Burned that whole damn village to the ground. I must have killed thirty of the bastards that day. I probably got the one that did that to him, we guess.' Swagger finished his beer and broke the back of another one. Then he raised it to the cripple, who looked on like a taxidermied hound, glass eyes raised admiringly. 'The best man I know,' he said, 'and they took his arm, the sons of bitches!' And he flung the glass of beer into the wall. _____ had been keeping pace, had been loosened by his whiskies and beers—he grabbed my glass of water from the table and flung it after Swagger's beer. 'SONS OF BITCHES,' he screamed, and went back to his own drink.

'You boys ever speak to your writer friend, Holcomb, about himself before he came to the city? The sort of people he knew?' Swagger asked. 'Back when he could still speak, of course.'

'Sounds like a good war,' said _____.

'It was a hell of a war,' said Swagger wistfully. 'You ever been to war, Box? You look like you could be some use in a war.' I had nothing to say to that, but it didn't matter because he carried on talking. 'Evelyn Heydt,' he said. 'I understand that she owes some money.'

_____ didn't say anything.

'Well let's say she does, just for talking. That's not a thing that concerns us. Let's say she caught it off Holcomb. I know women who've caught worse things off me in the past.' He grinned at Childs and got a dutiful smirk back. 'And let's further say that Holcomb isn't in much of a condition to be earning a wage as anything but paste right now. That also doesn't concern us. Hell, could be he deserved it—I know plenty that do. There's not enough rods in this city for all the shooting it would take to clean it up. Heydt, Holcomb. None of that matters to us. I'm just interested in you boys. You boys do damn fine work.' His drink tipped back. 'Hell, I'm getting us another,' he said. _____ went with him. I was left with Childs staring at me.

Now he leaned across, pushing the stump of his shoulder into me, his breath itching my face.

He said, 'If you know what's good for you, you won't get involved.' He kept his voice low and his eyes on me. I thought that the way his stump was, we must have looked like a magic trick, like he'd pushed an arm clean through me.

'But then,' he said, 'what are you saving yourself for?' He looked at me, but not like he was expecting anything, and then went back to circling the top of his glass with a finger.

Swagger and _____ came back carrying drinks, and Childs sat back in his chair. They hadn't brought me any water.

They filled and overfilled and refilled themselves with drinks. Swagger was telling another war story. About a time Childs had dived on top of a grenade. 'He saved my goddamn life. That grenade blew both of his kidneys clean out of him,' he was saying. 'He still doesn't piss right. The best friend I have in the word. In the world. You boys are freelance, correct? I mean I know you do most of your work for . . . Danskin? Or . . . ?' He looked at _____ inquisitively, but he might as well have asked the faces in his billfold.

'The point is you do good work,' Swagger said. He'd been saying it all night. 'And maybe you're interested in being hired to do some more. We had a strange visitor to our office recently. Death himself, or at least, that's how he looked. As tall as Box here, but thin as a whip, and a face from a horror flick. I'm lucky I've got a hell of a tough secretary, because most would have fled or expired at the sight of him. He claimed to have known of Holcomb in a previous life. Previous to the one that's just been wrung out of him, I mean.'

He looked at us hard. _____ was listing back and forth in his seat—it was hard to know what he was hearing, whether it was Swagger or just the noises of the drunk sea he drifted on alone.

'Anyway,' Swagger said, 'this tall figure with the death's head, he set us on a piece of work, and I'd say we could use help.' He pulled out a business card and slid it face down across the table to _____. 'That's my address. If you're interested stop by some time tomorrow. Call before you do. Marly, a real doll—she'll take a message if I'm out. Might even be more interesting than breaking hands and fanning dead writers,' he said cheerfully and slapped _____ on the shoulder.

_____ had picked up the card and looked it over, and he tucked it into his pocket with a nod.

They drank until they could barely stand and Swagger's stories got caught in time, looping round and round, until _____ was howling and roaring more and more while they looped like it was a ride at the fairground, and Childs eyed me and nursed his beer, and I drank my water and wondered what it was all about.

Interlude

His yell as they throw him from the train still fails to compel itself on their minds. He tumbles between the tracks and, quicker even than the first, is out of sight.

Hector rattles the railing the man has just journeyed over. He tries to kick the rust from the barrier, the anger from his body. He wants to get off the train, but there's no way off, only the same hard way that two men have already taken, not for another fifty minutes or more, until they reach the city. He screams abuse at the night.

Charles smiles and enjoys his cigarette—Hector's frustration is another familiar external roar, like the roar of the train's engine, and it is making him feel calmer. Hector kicks and rattles at the railing. He throws his hat at the ground and shouts at Charles, screams directly up into his smile and the exhaust from his cigarette, 'You big incompetent lug, you colossal stupid try-hard sa—' but he is interrupted by the hat, which skitters towards the back of the train, aiming for its own death plunge, flapping into the bars of the railing, and Hector skitters after it, making Charles roar now, with laughter. Hector pulls the hat down firmly onto his head and looks at him.

'Christ, what is there to be sour about?' asks Charles.

'You expect so little from the world,' says Hector,

'because you engage with it on a desultory level. You have no teeth, no hooks, no grip, so when life provides disappointments, you are content. You're an insect so unburdened by any weight of thought that it can move on top of water and live on drifting scum. Yes, I'm sour. I'm sour at him'—he points back—'because we gave him every chance and he provided us with so little.'

'And so then what? It's done, it's passed,' says Charles. 'The man's gone. In the sense that we threw him clean from existence, and in the just as absolute sense that he's already miles back, and we have to continue forward.'

'Continue forward for what?'

Charles taps Hector on the left breast pocket, where there is a letter from a woman Hector met at her wedding, though he doesn't remember her, who now has a man that she wants killed. 'Besides,' says Charles, 'the impulse is hardly exhausted. As an experiment, he was disappointing, of course, but there are other ways to proceed.'

Hector wants to get the job done with and over, Charles wants to have a good night's rest after the journey, and in the morning make their trip to the nuthouse. But mainly he wants to go and get tight, so they go into a bar across from the train station and set about getting tight.

'There's never been a job with less urgency to it,' Charles says, which is true, and Hector is only a little sore at being made to waste time.

They order food and sit beside a window to eat it. As

they're finishing their meal, a prowl car making a turn mounts the sidewalk next to them. They can see the two policemen inside: the one in the passenger seat presses his arm against the roof of the car to steady himself as it drops off the curb again. It comes to a stop in front of the train station. They watch the policemen go inside.

'So,' says Charles, 'what did we think of the two performances on the train?'

'We said already,' says Hector. 'They gave it their all, or we gave it their all, but the result was unspectacular.'

'There was no charge to it. We can mope about that, we can say that these were unremarkable men, gave unremarkable performances and perished, but then what? In that situation, whose is the lack of commitment?'

'They gave it their all,' says Hector.

'They gave it their all,' says Charles, 'so don't we owe it to them to continue to think this through?'

'I'm unmoved by the suggestion that we owe them anything,' says Hector and gives a squeak of a belch.

Charles proceeds, keeping irritation, with some effort, to the outside edge of his voice. 'We don't owe them anything, but to leave things as they are is to cement our disappointment. If we can accept the little they provided it becomes all that we deserve. Or.'

'Or?'

'Or what succeeds them might still justify their performances,' says Charles.

'You have a suggestion,' says Hector.

'I have a suggestion,' says Charles. 'Compel the next one to create a persona. The last gave us his own story and it was nothing.'

'Trite.'

'Trite, uninteresting, unmemorable. There was no charge. Let's say that the next is called—'

'Earl,' suggests Hector.

'Earl. But we sit him down and make him tell us he's called—'

'Douglas.'

'Douglas. And he's employed as a gas station attendant, but we make him tell us he's a—'

'Plumber.'

'Whatever you want,' says Charles. 'The thing would be to get an account of the life, as we did from'—he's lighted a new cigarette and he points it in the direction of the prowl car and the station—'Ed back there. Except that this life will not at all resemble the actual lived experience. It would be a fiction, a deceit. Now would that make us feel any differently about Douglas's subsequent victimhood than we do about Ed's?'

'It might,' shrugs Hector.

'Might it even illuminate how we feel about Ed's victimhood? Might we re-conceive the loss to his two children of a caregiver and model for male adulthood, the loss to Charlotte of a lover, to his employer of an obviously intelligent, committed man? We would have more information about our response to the factual account by having had another response to a fraud.'

'The man's name,' says Hector, 'wasn't Ed, whatever it was, and the other details are just as wrong.'

Charles grinds his teeth. 'I don't know why you're pretending to be too dense to take my point. It allows us to proceed to a new experience in a way that might also go some way to redeeming the old.'

'I suppose it might colour things,' says Hector.

PART 4

'Mike Swagger, Private Detective' was painted on the glass of the door. Childs' name didn't appear.

We went in to a small anteroom, where a woman who must have been Marly sat behind her desk smiling sweetly. We took our hats off. _____ coughed into his hand and then used it to press down his hair. We walked over to her. She smiled. 'Mike told me all about you both. Thank you so much for coming in.'

She spoke sweet and low, a sashay of a voice. There are those who say they've heard the voice of God, and I've never wondered what that would be like, but it occurred to me that there was nothing God could say that Marly's voice couldn't keep him in bed an hour longer.

'Please go on. Mike won't be busy for long.'

_____ opened the door through to the inner office and inside Swagger was sitting at his desk, in conversation with a man, standing, who twitched nervously at our entrance—who looked like he twitched nervously at everything. Swagger gestured for us to sit in some green leather padded chairs by the door and we sat and waited, our hats in our laps.

'Yes, it's a little jail time, Terrence,' Swagger was saying, 'but that's still a hell of a deal for you. We both know with a bit more sniffing around they could light you up like a firework, so why not make this easy for all of us and take the time? Sit it out. You've done it before, told me you taught yourself some Spanish when you were in. How's your Spanish now, Terrence?'

'I'm not going to jail!' Terrence screeched back. He had the stringy build of a snow fiend, his shirt was untucked, and from the back of his pants stuck a revolver that looked like it weighed twice what he did. Now he grabbed it and started waving it about, though it was shy about pointing directly at Swagger. I looked over at ____ and he shrugged. We sat and watched. 'I'm not going to no jail! You hear me, you flatfoot? I'm not going to jail over this.' The gun was shaking in his hand like he was already rattling at his bars. Swagger sighed, slid open a drawer and lifted out his own gun. He placed it on the desk, but kept one hand on it.

'Terrence,' he said, 'another day I'd have laid you flat already, but I'm in a good mood. I got guests here. Marly's wearing the sweater I got her for her birthday, and it suits her. But there's no way for you to walk away from this but you put down the gun. And then you've got to go to jail. Sit out your time. Everyone from heaven to hell and on down to the local police station knows you earned it.'

'You ever had a chance to lay me flat you'd have done it,' shouted Terrence, his big gun drawing a jittery outline around Swagger.

'I've had chances before, Terrence,' said Swagger

178

calmly. 'You know what I haven't had before? The law on my side. But as long as you're waving that gat around I can put as many bullets in you as I like, and they're not going to take away my P.I. ticket, not even going to ask me how to spell your name properly, I bet. You're just another scuzzball got taken out in the course of my peerless investigative work.'

_____ tapped me on the leg. He wanted me to look at a picture hanging on the wall. It was a handsomely framed photograph of Mike Swagger. Swagger was tipping his hat back with the barrel of his Colt .45 to show off his smile to the camera. It was nicely lit. He had signed it.

Behind the desk, with the same gun in front of him, Swagger continued negotiations. 'Instead of that you're going to put the gun down, we're going to work out a confession for you to sign, and I'm going to make sure that they don't so much as caress a bruise onto you on your way to the cells. Okay Terrence?'

'No,' said Terrence. 'I can't sign no confession. They told me they'd p-pull out my throat, they'd kill me if I said one word to the cops.'

'P-pull out your throat? Kill you?' Swagger asked. He sighed. 'Well, I guess I can't raise it,' he said, 'but I'll match it.'

Terrence's gun rattled some more. Swagger smiled at us flatly from the wall: the one behind the desk looked more stubbled, tired, aggrieved. _____ yawned and crossed his legs.

Finally Swagger lost patience. 'Goddammit Terrence,' he said and his chair went back, the gun came up, and the barrel threw a blast of fire toward the ground, where it went through the coke's foot, and he went down howling. Swagger came round the table to the loud mess on the floor, and gargled its cries by pressing his foot against its neck. 'What do you need a throat for anyway, Terrence? This is the most I ever heard you say for Christ's sake.' Then he heeled it away, disgusted, and picked up the abandoned revolver. 'I didn't need another hole in my floor, Terrence,' he said. Then, to us: 'Sorry about this, boys, won't take a second now.'

_____ smiled, like he was having enough fun now not to mind waiting.

Swagger dragged the mewling Terrence with his punc-tured foot through to the anteroom by the hair. _____ and I got up to watch. Marly was standing watching too. She didn't seem to be finding it too unusual a show. Swagger cuffed the coke to a handle of a filing cabinet. Terrence was weeping curses and Swagger told him to keep it clean, and in a moment of hurt, angry clarity the coke managed to spit two words at Swagger, the second 'off'. As he was saying it Swagger's fist connected, slamming his head to the cabinet, and before Terrence dropped, Swagger had caught his head in both hands and lowered him like the head was a bowling ball and he was in his run up. He left Terrence slumped on the ground with one arm held up by the handcuff, looking like he hadn't been able to decide whether to pass out or hail a taxi.

'Sorry about that, kitten,' Swagger said to Marly.

She smiled demurely. It was a hell of a smile.

Swagger came back in the room and sat down, slapping his hands on the desk and looking at us like we were a feast laid out for him. 'Pull those chairs over here!' he said. We dragged them closer, with some effort and a fair amount of noise, which drew Swagger's eyes down to the floor, and for a moment he looked sombre. 'That punk,' he said. 'Blood and holes. My floor doesn't need it.' But his cheer came back to him quickly. 'Childs should be here soon. Let me fill you in, though all on the QT, you understand.' He took a cigar from a box, bit the end from it, took a lighter the size of a railcar from his desk and ignited it. He blew a couple of large, soft clouds.

'Used to be this town was lousy with dicks,' he said. 'So much competition you could hardly shake up enough business to get by, but that's not the case any more. The city's low. It's good for business, sure, but it's a problem when you're a couple of hands short and could use an extra gum-heel. Childs and me thought you boys might fill a need, as it were.' He turned the cigar in his hand as he spoke. 'There's a case. More angles to this thing than the two of us together can keep on top of. More angles than a geometry textbook.' He grinned at both of us in turn, making sure we got that one. 'We need someone we can trust to go knock on some doors. Nothing complicated, just take a couple of names, maybe ask a couple of questions and report back on the parties involved, be our eyes and ears on the ground.'

There came the noise of the outer office door. We turned awkwardly round in our chairs to see Childs come through from the anteroom. He took position by Swagger's desk. As Swagger talked, Childs reached across his body and took a pouch from beneath his missing arm, then laid it on the desk, took a paper from it and started piling it with tobacco.

'There's a strange bird in town. A Frenchman, by the name of Lowden,' Swagger continued. 'Or he says that's what he's called. Clarence Lowden, as in Lowden Cosmetics.'

Lowden Cosmetics made creams, lipsticks, perfumes: stuff so expensive you'd almost believe it could do all they promise. Ruin marriages or save them, depending on your preference. Stop ageing for good. Turn back the wind.

'Clarence is the son and heir. All you have to do is confirm he is who he says he is. The case we're working on, there are certain financial benefits that might accrue to Lowden, depending on how it all plays out,' Swagger said. 'You'll go to the apartment straight from here. You don't need to alarm Mr Lowden, it's not that kind of job. And don't worry about being seen, that's fine, you're legit now,' he said. 'You don't even necessarily need to speak with him.'

Childs turned the cigarette he'd been making with practised delicacy, twisting an end. He put the pill in his mouth and a match from somewhere sparked on the inside of his thumbnail. As he lighted the twist of paper the stump of his shoulder raised in sympathy, moving the ghost of a hand to shield the flame.

'If this Lowden's a phoney . . .' Swagger let the consequences drift in the smoky air. He took his big feet from his desk and tossed a slim brown file into _____'s lap. 'That's a handwriting sample from the real Lowden.' _____ looked at it with glittering eyes like this was as good as tickets to the circus. 'We don't know what the real Lowden looks like, so that's how you're going to tell.'

They walked with us most of the way to Lowden's, while _____ kept his arms wrapped around the file, clutching it to his chest. Then Swagger reminded _____ of our instructions, and they breezed.

The building slumped, half-sized between its neighbours: they looked like they had it by the shoulders, ready to sling it into traffic. _____ pressed the bell marked 'Fischer' and when the lock buzzed we went up. Fischer met us through a door that stayed chained. He looked us up and down like he was going to be measuring us for suits, then passed Lowden's key. 'Don't bring it back here,' he said. 'I don't want to know any more about it.'

We took the key along to Lowden's. The apartments didn't look like the sort that might house an heir to anything more desirable than rheumatism. When there was no answer to our knocks we let ourselves in.

There was a wall bed that was up. There were a couple of chairs for receiving guests and one more beside a small flat-topped desk. There was a trunk pressed against the wall. There was a body on the floor.

Fat Lowden had his eyes peacefully closed, his face a beautiful sky blue, one blue cheek pressed into the carpet. His rear-end was up in the air, so from his knees to his head he made a triangle packed with his big, round gut. His arms were splayed out and his neck was corrugated, the same as Holcomb's had been. He was in the very middle of the room, like he was on display, like he was art. He looked like a hermit crab stripped of its shell.

_____ gave an angry grunt, and for a moment looked like he was going to give the corpse a kick, but instead he started searching the room. He took the drawers from the desk and threw them on the ground. The first was empty, in the second a single long, brass screw rattled. He pulled down the wall bed, and when that didn't achieve anything he pulled off the sheets. Then he threw the bed up, banging it against the wall, screaming at it, banging it again.

Lowden had bare feet. I looked around for his shoes. They were lying neatly by the desk.

Meanwhile _____ was trying to lift the lid of the trunk but the whole trunk came with it, jumping clear of the ground, like it was trying to buck him. _____ was looking for something Lowden had written on. Something he could use to compare with the sample Swagger had given him. He'd been given a handwriting sample and now he'd been cheated out of it. He took out his knife, jammed it in the lock of the trunk and tried to force it, but got nowhere. He flung the knife into the carpet. He screamed, cursed, and then he did kick Lowden, right at the pitch of the triangle, and it seemed like it lifted him a full inch off the ground then put him back down in the same ridiculous position, his blue face as serene as ever, his head a deflating balloon.

I started checking Lowden's trouser pockets. I took out a keyring with six keys on it, and a metal comb. Then _____ grabbed the dead man's jacket and I had to stand clear. _____ started ripping it off him, shaking the body out of it, and then shaking everything from the pockets. There was a large handkerchief that flapped fragrantly into the room, some coins, a platinum watch on a chain, a fountain pen, an ivory sheaf of engraved cards, and a nearly empty package of violet pastilles. _____ roared with dissatisfaction, his hands on his head, his eyes wide and furious. While _____ was rending his hair I looked at the cards that were spilling from the sheaf. They said 'Clarence Lowden'. It didn't matter.

_____ took the keyring and went back to the trunk. The second key he tried opened it. I went over and stood with him as he burrowed through the layers of smartly folded clothes and towels. At the bottom, beside a .25 automatic with a walnut handle and a box of ammunition, was a stack of Hotel New Europe writing paper. _____ flung himself on the paper, found it was blank and threw it in disgust. He grabbed Lowden by his shirt and shook him like he was going to make him talk, then punched him hard, knocking his nose sideways. There wasn't any blood. The dead don't bleed much: they've aged out of it.

Finally _____ grabbed the pen and jammed it into Lowden's hand, his own hands encasing the dead man's like he was bringing comfort to him too late, then he pushed the pen down onto a sheet of the paper, trying to make a loop or a line that he might match against the ones in Swagger's sample, but the paper bent into the carpet and tore, and _____'s hands tightened in anger, and a snapping came from Lowden's dead fingers. _____ roared angrily again, then finally seemed spent. He kneeled on the carpet with his head down so there were two penitents, one blue and silent, the other red and panting.

After a time _____ said calmly—like it was the most obvious, quietly tedious thing in the world—that we had been wasting our time. And then stood up and wiped the hair back from his brow.

We were near a place where _____ liked the milkshakes, and by the time he had finished a milkshake a lot of his anger had left him. Then we went back to Swagger's to tell the shamus what we'd found.

Behind the communicating door to Swagger's office there was only darkness—Marly told us he'd left a message saying we should come by again the next day, anytime before noon. It sounded so nice the way she said it that _____ had her tell us again. Then _____ let her know that her boss had sent us visiting with a corpse.

She looked gingerly thoughtful, like he'd offered to buy her a drink and she was considering it. Maybe this was how she always looked in grief. 'You might want the buttons involved,' _____ said. He got no reaction. He shrugged. We turned to go.

'See you in the morning, boys,' she said, and her voice lapped at us like the tide.

Like a lovesick young pup _____ went back to the same dive where we'd been drinking with Swagger the night before.

I wasn't in the mood to watch him drink, and if the dialogue-heavy gumshoe did show, then I knew I wouldn't be in the mood to listen. But I needed somewhere to be. This is always the thing, this is the tide we can't not swim against—that we all always have to find somewhere to be. You chew down the tiredness until it chokes you, you keep finding somewhere to be until you're excused, finally. Like Lowden had been excused. Like Holcomb had.

If I was going to carry on being somewhere, I decided it would be Evelyn Heydt's. _____ had already forgotten her: he'd found a place to be, for now, and it was sniffing at the heels of Swagger, hoping he'd get given a chance to have a hand grenade blow out his kidneys, or be passed another handwriting sample.

I hadn't forgotten her.

I had the thought that the place I wanted to be was with

her, and it sent me tumbling into a well of myself—I found she'd been swimming around in there, a great shoal of welcome thoughts, had been there ever since we'd been in her apartment, ever since we'd seen her standing at her window, beautiful and unaware. I'd been peering past her to watch _____ kick a fat corpse, to sit with him as he drank an angry milkshake, but now thoughts of Evelyn Heydt plunged together, filled my view, pushed out _____ and Swagger.

I was going to go and see Evelyn Heydt.

At every stop on the streetcar more and more people got on. I felt like I was at the bottom of a chute and men with ties and ladies with grocery bags and squabbling kids were being dropped onto me. I got pushed further, tighter to the back. Then the redheaded pickpockets got on. In a line they got on, paid their fares and moved into the car, one, two, three.

I watched them for the rest of the journey. They hadn't seen me. They talked, looking forward rather than at each other, and as the car started to empty out again they moved, almost marching, around one of the vertical metal poles, the same as the one I was holding on to.

The way they moved started to make me feel queasy, the way their movements matched each other. They moved like three bottles carried by the same wave. As one of them turned the pole he stretched his arm out and peeled away from it, and stepped a big, high-legged marching step to the window, his arm raised to a handle. Then the second followed behind: the same turn, same big step back to the window and arm raised. And then the third: the movements passing one to the other like a finger runs along the keys of a piano, and from where I was watching they disappeared, one behind the other, like they'd been stacked inside each other. Only when the streetcar went around a corner or reached a slope could I see that there was more than one of them, the three identical images spreading apart then resolving into each other again. It was as though seeing the first burned him into your eye, leaving other pale redheads ghosting behind. As they muttered and moved I watched how they raised their hands and turned their feet around other passengers, the beating of their lips, and I couldn't see a difference between them. I couldn't shake the feeling I was seeing the same moment three times. Then in sequence they left the streetcar.

Like three bows on a single kite string, one after the other.

Once, in a wooden hut by a rollercoaster, I'd seen a spinning toy lit by flashing lights. It was a cylinder of panels that showed a running horse with an Indian on his back, and the horse really did run, its legs drawn in pen but in flickering movement, as the cylinder spun and the flashing light controlled the time, taking the individual moments and making them into a single, living scene, until the spinning slowed, and the horse separated into shuddering, sliding parts.

When the triplets had left, a woman on the streetcar

with a kind voice asked me if I felt all right. I was shaking. I coughed some vomit into my hand, and she didn't move from me, but gave me a handkerchief from her bag.

On the street, it was Marly I comforted myself with thoughts of as I cleaned my face and hand. Marly was a fixed point, something you'd want to keep: she was in it with Swagger, but a lot gets forgiven for that voice, those eyelashes, so however you approached things you'd want Marly to be there—at least to know she existed as a possibility, a warm thought to enjoy as you drift to sleep.

Holcomb I liked a lot less, but now I felt as if I needed him too. If I could I wanted to unwring his neck, slip his drooping eye back into place and pat down the big sagging bruise around it, to paste up the hole the bullet had drilled in his cheek and put his teeth back in his mouth like I was dropping nickels into a machine.

More than anything there was Evelyn Heydt. Beautiful, stage-lit Evelyn Heydt, beautiful and close, with her fluttering eyelids, her quickened, pulse-warmed cheek. To be back in that moment of pursuit, to be drawn towards her blood-red lips as they trembled, but with life, not fear.

I rinsed off the handkerchief with the overrun from a gutter.

I pressed three bell-buttons together, none of them Evelyn Heydt's. The lock of the street door buzzed and I went in and up the stairs.

I imagined: knocking, the door opening, her seeing the look in my eyes, screaming maybe, backing away, almost tripping in her terror. The whole scene playing out again. She would move back, scared, and I would move toward her like she was drawing me on a string. I would menace and she would retreat. And maybe it would end as it had before, with the big detective coming from nowhere to lay a sap on me, and her swept off in his arms. And maybe it wouldn't and no one would appear. Maybe Swagger was blind drunk in a bar with _____. Maybe he was sweeping other dames into his arms across the city, but not her. And maybe I'd scare her into giving up whatever money Holcomb had given her, or maybe I'd twist her neck and put a hole in her chin, and pull her place apart looking for it and the debt would keep moving and we'd follow after it.

I shook my head to get the rain from my hat. I put the hat under my arm. I took my raincoat off and held the hat in my hand and hung the coat across my forearm. I straightened my tie and wiped my face and neck with the handkerchief, and I tried to make the wet handkerchief a square for my breast pocket. Then again, but folded the other way. I hung the raincoat and hat on the banister and went over to the night-mirrored window. Imagine my face. I meant to do something to my hair, I raised my hands to do something but what do you do to hair? It felt wrong to beat up on it without a plan.

I turned around and Evelyn Heydt was looking at me

from her open door. I was somewhere now, but without an idea of what I meant to do there.

She looked a different person than she had the day before. She wasn't made of the same parts. I hadn't shaved.

I tried to say something, but I wasn't sure where the words led and I swallowed the first of them as it started to grow. She waited for me and something like concern took her. I could see it like she could see me struggling to make a word.

Before we'd waited for morning or for me to get a sentence out, she said, 'Is it about one of the girls? One of Danskin's girls? Is that why you've come?' And I looked like however I look when I don't know what someone means, but she opened the door to me and had me sit and sat with me.

We sat for a while, both waiting for me to say something. I teetered, like a child liable to fall from some small but significant height. I shook my head, no, to the question she'd asked at the door. 'We,' I said. 'It's,' I said. I swallowed and coughed and said, my voice only slightly flooded with air, only slightly broken, 'Hol comb. The writer.'

I told her that was why we'd come. That Holcomb died owing money.

I lighted a cigarette without dropping it. She moved some cushions around like she was stirring sugar in her tea. She had her hair tied back. Instead of the dress from the day before, she wore a white blouse tucked into a navy skirt. She said she knew him. She'd known he was in trouble but not how much. She asked if I knew him. I shook my head, no—I wanted to hear her speak, not to answer questions. She said it was sad and with a look she made it seem it.

I wanted to know how they'd met but I didn't know how to ask it. The first way I tried it, before the first word was all the way out I realised I was asking more than I meant—as if I was asking her how long they had been together, or if she was with someone else. I caught the word but not a sort of gasping cluck, and I tried again and the same thing happened. And she looked at me and there was something like surprise or curiosity—at seeing me foolish and clucking—but also sympathy and understanding.

'He came with a girl,' she said, 'the first time I met him. One of the girls from The Little Death. The girls from there know to come to us if they get in trouble. Not just from there, we'll always try and help anyone. Dr Boken, he's not involved, but we couldn't do it without access to the surgery, and the drugs, and he turns a blind eye to all of that.'

She looked at me curiously again. It could have been the look people give when they don't think you're understanding them, when they think you're not up to building with the bricks that they're passing you. I know that look. This was different—she was trying to see if I would use any of this in a way to hurt her. She said, 'If we don't help they end up going somewhere that it's dangerous for them. It's better they come to us. God knows it's not perfect, but it's clean.'

She asked for a cigarette and I handed her one from the pack.

She reached toward me and picked my cigarette from my lips. She put its lighted end to the unlit end of her own and inhaled, pulling the air back up through my cigarette, through its flame, which growled and chewed into the end of her cigarette—and then up through it, into herself.

She handed back the cigarette. We sat and smoked without saying anything. She seemed relaxed now. To sit with her was something.

'He was crazy, it turned out,' she said, with a smile. 'He was a writer, and I asked him about it once so he gave me a story he'd written. But when I told him I'd liked it, I must have said something wrong, because he started waving his hands around, and shouting. I had to watch him have a tantrum. It turned out he believed a lot of the nonsense he was writing. He kept shouting and flapping his arms, so I threw him out. Someone being crazy is one thing, but I'm not having a man come here to shout his craziness at me. I've had enough of shouting, I think.'

She flattened her cigarette in an ashtray. 'That would have been the last time I saw him, so I don't know what I can do for you,' she said. 'I don't have his money—I don't have much money of my own.'

*

I was going to ask about Swagger, how she had met him, and what she'd been doing missing work yesterday, and why she'd been all dressed up, why she'd been scared. But she stood and offered me coffee and I told her I'd like a glass of water and she left the room.

As soon as I was alone I got the feeling of being drawn forward, like sitting still was impossible, and I started to sweat. Money wasn't what this was about, but then I wasn't sure what it was about. I'd made it to Evelyn Heydt's on my own, but now I didn't know what I was doing there and there was no one to tell me. From her direction came the sound of a running tap, and hearing it tore a strip straight out of me. I jumped on a pencil and a magazine she had lying there. On the back cover was an advertisement: 'The road to pleasure is thronged with smokers who have discovered this better cigarette.' I wrote a note over the top of it. Next time I'd bring _____ along to get the money and things wouldn't go astray, then. Only things were already going astray, I looked at what I'd written and the two had slipped together—the advert and the note—so it read: 'The road to what plea-sure is thronged with Holcomb owed smokers who have you owe discovered this better cigarette.'

I dropped sweat all the way out the door, I pushed the magazine into my pocket, I got out of there.

In the street I left my hat off so the rain could cool my face.

_____ wasn't around when I got back to my mattress. He was out drinking or he was out rolling in the hay, whatever it was. I couldn't sleep. I just kept walking in circles like I was flattening the grass, thinking about Evelyn Heydt, and her knee almost close enough to touch mine. Evelyn Heydt taking my cigarette and pulling my breath back through it.

I went to Lydia's door, hoping there would be a light coming from it and I could talk to her. I'd missed talking to her, with the apartment manager still no one knew where, and her dirty jokes and everything lively in her gone with him.

There was no light, and I imagined her on the other side of the door, shrinking, shrinking smaller and further into her sheets until she was wrinkled and pale and more bed-sheet than she was person. I went to knock anyway—I couldn't imagine that she was asleep, because I couldn't imagine her sleeping, not the Lydia that she'd shrunk into, like I couldn't imagine her singing, or flying, or awake, so I didn't think I'd be disturbing her to knock. But then I didn't know what we could say to each other if she answered, so I didn't knock. I went and lay down.

I fell asleep, I must have, because _____ woke me: the noise of him pissing so loud it sounded like it was striking the mattress beside my head.

And I fell asleep again, because it was morning and Swagger shaking our door almost to parts woke the two of us.

I pulled on a shirt and went to the door while _____ tried to cough himself awake, rattling phlegm from his cage. Swagger talked clear around me to _____, preferring to speak to the man coughing in another room than the man who'd opened the door to him. He said loudly, 'There's another job for you. Another strange bird to find, name of Cansel.'

_____ called back that Lowden was dead.

Swagger took that as an invitation to come in. 'Don't worry about Lowden,' he said. 'Not many people are going to miss him. You did exactly what you were meant to do.'

We dressed and he walked with us to the Ambassador Hotel. 'You're going to wait in the lobby,' he said to _____. 'Wait there until you see me come and give you the nod, then you go up to Cansel's room. He's in room 222. Room . . .' He stopped walking as his voice tailed off. He turned to _____.

'222,' said _____.

We started walking again. 'Room 222,' said Swagger. 'Jean Cansel will be out, but he's travelling with a large trunk, and it's the trunk we're interested in. You go up to the room, but take the stairs, not the elevator, and you say nothing to anybody about why you're there. Once you're in, check the trunk for a package. You ever seen a baby wrapped up so tight it looks like it just came in the mail? This is going to be that size, but a lot more precious.'

We'd reached the Ambassador. Swagger lighted another cigar. 'You'll know it when you see it,' he said. 'No need to open it, just take it and leave the same way you came. Go take a seat, boys.' As we went into the hotel he called out, 'Room 222, boys.'

We sat in the elegantly crumpled seats in the lobby. They were this kind of seat: you sank into them for a long time, like you were a grand old ocean liner, and they smelled so good I could hardly bear it.

An old man—crumpled, but not so elegantly—sat nearby, busily attending to not watching us with the aid of a newspaper. This was the house peeper. His shoulder rig and his hairline were both too high. We watched him. We watched him without the subterfuge with which he watched us. We watched him and he boiled under it. In less than the time it took for the band on the radio to change song, his bottom lip was slick with sweat.

Whether Swagger appeared and gave his nod or not, we would get to sit watching this old house peeper, with a well-combed moustache and a holster that had never been separated from its gun, and it felt good. We watched him for as long as it took _____ to smoke three cigarettes. We watched him for so long he had, finally, to do something about it.

He folded his newspaper and walked over to us tapping it against his leg. He coughed. He asked us if we were waiting for somebody or maybe we were just keeping out of the rain. His moustache twitched like a car veering into oncoming traffic. He knew he'd waited a long time before asking us and the cowardliness bothered him.

_____ grinned and extinguished his current cigarette in the ash stand by his seat.

I stood and the peeper took a half-step back and I matched him. He said something that turned into a burst of tuts and gasps, like his tongue was tumbling down the back of his throat, and shuffled like he was thinking of reaching for his gun.

I grabbed onto his jacket with my left hand, and the holster and the gun with it, wadding it all in place.

The peeper's fingers slipped wetly around mine. He tried to take another step back and I held him where he was. He didn't swing at me or look me in the eye or give any clue that he thought I had anything to do with why he couldn't get a hold of his gun, why he wasn't getting to act like a man ought to act, why he couldn't keep charge of his own hotel lobby.

_____ was at my side. While the peeper shivered in my grip, he began unfolding his knife from his pocket and its handle. He did it slowly, while the peeper's eyes darted from it to me—anxious, pleading—and to his fumbling hands on the wad of suit where the gun was fixed.

Then there was Swagger, inserting himself between me and the peeper like he was cutting in to take the next dance.

'You're looking a little rattled, Glenn,' Swagger said. 'You holding it together? A hotel dick's got to look the part or people start to talk.' And like that I'd been eased off—a piece of meat peeled from the griddle. _____ tipped his knife into itself and returned it to its pocket, and Swagger moved the peeper back to arm's length, and we stood like a group of friends well on the way to becoming good acquaintances.

The hotel dick wiped his brow and his chin with his pocket square and tried to climb his tongue back up into his mouth using the other detective's name for steps. 'Mike, Mike,' he said, 'it's good to see you, Mike.'

'Always good to see you, Glenn, and to visit a high-class establishment like this, where I've never seen so much as a lick of trouble and never expect to neither. And these two boys,' Swagger said, turning to us, laying his arm around the wilted hotel detective, 'do you know these two boys?'

'N-no, Mike,' said the peeper, finally with the courage to look at us angrily, a couple of heels, lousing up his lobby.

'Well, they look like they've probably got some business to attend to, don't you, boys?' Swagger leaned forward. He loomed. He was meaningful. 'Don't you have some business to attend to, boys?'

We walked as if to leave. Behind the reception a skinny, fair-skinned boy—open-mouthed, with an Adam's apple like a doorknob—watched us, had been watching the whole thing without ever having a thought to do anything but watch. Swagger whistled a note and called him over by name and the kid trotted past us in his direction. Swagger had already sat his friend Glenn with his back to us, so with the kid gone, we just kept walking past the exit and up the stairs.

_____ popped the lock of room 222 with his knife.

We saw Cansel immediately. He was in the bed, covered with a sheet.

Immediately we knew it—before we even saw the bloody stain, we knew. It wasn't, I guess, hard to know by then. I closed the door. _____ pressed his hands to his eyes. He cursed joylessly. We were getting the corpse tour of the city: come and see it, lifeless worthless death. Let the bodies pile up: Holcomb, Lowden, Cansel. Everywhere we walked our path was already flat and dead, and I was sick of walking it.

Cansel's body made a long, low mound in the bedsheet. The sheet was pulled up past the top of his head, pulled up so far that feet in expensive shoes stuck from the bottom end. The blood made an oval like a red rug that hung off one side of him, stuck to his gut by two darker red pits the size of ashtrays.

We walked toward him.

_____ stood at one corner of the bed and I stood at another and between us were Cansel's feet, sticking from their shroud. _____ positioned a cigarette in his fingers by tapping it against the closer shoe.

The mound coughed and there was a crack like an

explosion from the bed that clapped across my ears and knocked all sense out of me.

The bed was on fire. The bloody mound was on fire—it had coughed and now it was on fire. One part of the sheet, the part that was on fire, was waving around, was a long arm, waving, it held a gun. The explosion, the shot, had rung a gong in my head, rung an impossibly high note, insistent and central. The arm was flailing—it held the fire, though the fire was spreading. We had both crouched as though we had thought for an instant to run. The high note drilled at me from inside but it was fading. Cansel's body was trying to shake loose the burning sheet, but he was caught in it and screaming. He rolled and his arm shook, and the sheet moved down his face, just far enough that we could see his eyes, which were wide and angry. We stood up from our crouch and watched him flail. The flapping arm, lengthened by the gun, was like a wing made of a flame that grew with every beat. Cansel's body screamed and rolled from side to side, but he was still caught, and a lot of the bed was burning, covered in flapping flames.

_____ put the cigarette in his mouth and lifted a match to light it. There was a second explosion from the long arm, again we had our hands to our ears, we crouched like we might run, and the shot knocked apart some of a bed post.

_____ was quick. He screamed at the screaming Cansel, and made for him. He had dropped his cigarette and his knife was out. He stabbed it into the mound, his arm dashing into the flame, punching with the little blade. He put one hand over the wide eyes and with the other drove the knife into the sheet and the covered head.

Cansel's screams became louder and filled with water and then stopped as _____ stabbed at the head and neck through the pattern of slits, the red mouths he'd already cut. I had moved closer, to stop him or to help, and I put a hand out toward him. The sleeve of _____'s jacket caught the fire and he reeled, his knife slicing my palm. He got the jacket off and beat it against the still, heavy mound that had been Cansel until there was no more fire anywhere.

There wasn't much smoke, but it carried the smell of Cansel's burning.

The blood spread and soaked round the cuts in the head and neck of the shroud, and the sheet clung closer until we could make out features—the angle of Cansel's cheek-bone, the rise of his nostrils, the long coastline of his open mouth—all cast in rich red.

There was no trunk, no package like a tightly wrapped baby.

A knock came from the wall by the head of Cansel's bed, at about the place of the open-mouthed red mask that lay there, as if they were rapping on his skull to wake him. And then three more knocks. Someone shouted, indistinctly. They hadn't shouted before, unless they had been shouting while Cansel was screaming and the gong's high tone was vibrating through our heads. _____ yelled back, cursed at the voice, indistinctly too, and there was another knock, this one from the door.

_____ came around the bed to get Cansel's gun. The skin of Cansel's arm had melted to the sheet and _____ separated them with difficulty. There was a long .38 in Cansel's grip. _____ took the handkerchief from my pocket—the one the woman in the streetcar had given me. He used it to pick the hot gun out from Cansel's fingers.

The knock at the door came again and now a voice called for Mr Cansel. He didn't answer.

I thought about opening the door, letting whoever was outside into the room, to see what would happen. Something to get us off this dead path, so there would be no more getting sent by Swagger to inspect corpses or kill them again while they screamed at us with wide eyes. I was sick of it. But I put the chain on the door. And I went to the window, which was large and already partway open. As I pushed it all the way up, my left hand slipped from the blood on my fingers and I jarred my elbow hard against the window frame. I'd been cut, I remembered. Out of the window it was maybe a five-metre drop to the roofs of a line of off-duty cabs. I showed _____.

There was another knock on the door, but no louder, and another shout for Mr Cansel, another shout just as low on courage. It was the same hesitant half-voice from the hotel lobby—the voice of the hotel peeper, still unsteady on its feet. He was waiting. He'd wait until the prowl car boys arrived if he could. We had time.

_____ tossed the gun back onto the bed and put himself through the window so the right half of him tipped into the open air while the left half wriggled in a hotel room where a man had just been burned and stabbed. He turned his body around so he hung attached to the building by his fingertips. Then he dropped onto the hack beneath. He managed it quietly, gracefully even. The sounds of a conversation came from the corridor: the hotel dick explaining to someone, one of Cansel's neighbours maybe, why it would be indiscreet just to open up the door and see what was going on in the room, whatever the noise, however bad the smell was.

I followed _____ through the window.

I landed badly, denting the roof of the hack and bending my ankle as I tipped hard onto my side, my hip going into the hood, my shoulder into the windshield, and then fell, kept falling, off the hood and into the ground.

_____ helped me to my feet, he picked up my hat and brushed gravel from my knees with it, windshield glass from my shoulder. I was sick of it all and my knees hurt and I could have been anywhere else. I grabbed _____ by his lapels and shook him. He hung there, not objecting, and I shook him again.

My voice was bad. It comes and goes and it was bad now. I was filled with an anger I hadn't noticed grow.

I said, 'He's go ing to keep push ing us a round.'

The vocal chords, what happens is that they can't close,

so air escapes through the voice. When it's bad I sound like a leaky bellows. It tremors too, when it's bad.

I shook _____. I said, 'He will p ush us a round until we 're spent, then hand us to the buzz ers.' I breathed, and shook at _____ some more. 'And they 'll light us up.' I put _____ down so I could put my hands around the pain in my neck. I bent toward the ground and he laid a hand on my back. I could feel the blood from my cut hand running into the collar of my shirt, and I'd lost my mind, I was done with it all.

I shook his hand from my back and stood straight, taking my hands from the pain. 'I get lit up,' I said, 'it's go ing to be for some thing I chose.'

When the voice gets bad the struggle with it reaches my eyes too.

I took a while to breathe. _____ waited. There was still no one with us in the alley, no one at the window.

I said, 'I've got some where else I w ant to be,' and left him.

After that I went and got the small folding shovel _____ kept under his sink, and dug up the box of money I kept buried in the scrubland at the back of the building. I got dirt in my cut, but I didn't feel like taking the time to deal with it. I took the money.

Bernard took me in to see Fylan as soon as I asked, no objections, which was white of him. First Fylan said, 'You're going to scare the marks, coming in here looking like you look, Box. Go home,' but I shook my head, no, and he moved from watching the tables through his office door and told me to sit down. He poured me a whisky from a bottle in his desk into a little paper cup like a dentist would give you to rinse your mouth.

'You know you've got dirt and blood on your collar?' he asked. 'You cut yourself shaving? I always took you for part golem.' I took the little paper cup and drank it down. Sitting made me wince. I had to lay the leg straight out, the leg I'd twisted in the fall.

Fylan sighed. He opened a drawer and then a second and a third before he found a roll of gauze. He came round and took my cut hand from my lap and put it palm up on top of his leg. He wrapped it and folded the bandage into itself so it held. Then he sat again, poured himself a paper cup of whisky and said, 'What is it, Box? Where's _____?'

I said, 'I 've got the mo ney that Hol comb owed.'

At Evelyn Heydt's she took one look at the state of my collar and my hand and—without asking why I'd come, without shock, with only kindness in her voice—offered me her bathroom to clean myself up.

I washed the cut and the blood and dirt from myself as well as I could and then refitted Fylan's bandage. There wasn't much I could do about the shirt, but the water was good and hot and it steamed the mirror and made my face shine pink and bright.

When I came out she laughed at the bandage and did it again, did it right.

We sat together and I didn't feel any of the pull away from her, forwards and out of her apartment, back to _____. I was sharing time with her—and now there was no panic, nowhere the feeling that I was sitting outside an empty room looking in. Instead we were exactly what we seemed to be: two people in a room together, talking. And she was exactly what she had seemed to be: kind and beautiful. She talked to me easily, as if she was used to finding me at her door, as if she was used to doing kindnesses for me.

I asked her about her job and she talked to me about it. She seemed to know everything there was to know about teeth. There's a lot to know about teeth, you'd be surprised. She asked to see mine and then frowned when I showed them to her. I must have looked pretty worried, because she laughed at me then, too. She got me to open my mouth again and then she tapped on one of my teeth. She said it was squint. If it was pulled the rest would have more space and it would all straighten out. 'Don't get it pulled though,' she said. 'I like your smile. You shouldn't change it.' My smile was big and dumb and I couldn't stop it, not for minutes.

I sat with Evvie and I thought how I wanted to be there, not just then, but whenever I could be useful to her. I wanted to be there when there was nothing for us to do or say, and I wanted that to be long lazy years. The world could keep screwing itself deeper into all that nothingness unattended. I wanted to watch beside her eyes as her laugh wore wrinkles there—it would be a good way to spend the time, to see the things she might laugh at become a part of her beauty.

And I didn't need to say any of this, to struggle out a breathy, painful word of it. Like a miracle, she knew it. Somehow the good thoughts burned bright enough to be seen through all the rest of me, and she let me take her hand into mine and we sat like that, hand in hand.

I found myself remembering things I hadn't thought about for a long time, and I sat there remembering them, forgetting where I was. I remembered being in a car with _____, though I couldn't remember where we had got the car or where we were taking it, but _____ was driving and he drove very well. There was a peacefulness to him while he was driving. He was driving so smoothly, so gracefully, that I wanted to see if, without looking, I could feel when we were turning a corner, when we came to a stop, so I closed my eyes. Except I fell asleep, in the car, and I fell asleep in the memory too.

Evvie woke me. She was standing over me, and I guess I looked pretty content laid out on her couch because she had a curious, playful look on her face. She saw I'd woken and said, 'Hello there, happy bear.'

She said I was going to have to leave and she was going to go to bed. I said the next time I was going to come round

I'd call her first, and she gave a small, quick nod of agreement. I smiled big at that, a smile all over my face all at once like an egg cracked into a pan. I got her to kiss me on the cheek at the door, and she did, kissed me once on the cheek, and then I got her to kiss me quick on the lips, and without much of even a second's hesitation, I got my kiss, and before I could even smile she had closed the door.

I went to the New Europe, where I knew the peeper. He said I couldn't stay there unless I put on a clean collar, and he lent me one, and we sat and listened to the radio. He was too earthly tired even to speak much by then. He was glad when I went upstairs to sleep and left him to his tiredness.

The next day I began to find out what had happened to _____. That he had gone with Swagger and Childs and there'd been some shooting. That _____ had been out in the middle of the street and that he had his back to Swagger, when Swagger shot him twice, and that was the end.

Interlude

In a single movement, Charles loops the wire over the man's head, turns so that the two of them are back to back, and pulls hard, his hands together and each gripping a leather-wrapped handle of the wire, the base of his thumbs braced against his left clavicle. He bends forward at the waist, so that the other man is hoisted by the wire at the neck, becoming a wriggling, rasping sack that Charles is carrying over one shoulder. Hector sits in the darker corner of the back room, no more than a metre away. The wire has slipped through the skin in the man's neck and, as his legs bicycle and his body swings across Charles' wide back, Charles can feel the wire sawing through his throat, up and into the cartilage of the Adam's apple, then the jerk as it enters deep into the larynx, carving an entrance for blood to flow into the lungs and adding to the quiet flailing noise in the back room of this bar some of the sounds of drowning. When it's over Charles lays the new corpse down on the floor.

'Should I applaud?' asks Hector.

Charles wipes his brow: the work has made him sweat. 'Only if you feel moved to,' he says.

'I don't,' says Hector. 'Not your fault. This whole trip so far has been a tour of dissatisfaction.'

'Yes,' says Charles.

A tour of dissatisfaction: nothing excites them. The woman who they had talked to: when all pretence (on their side) had been dropped, and she was lying to them about the dimensions of her life, inventing her name, children, home town: the dissatisfaction arrived before even the conclusion. Hector suspected the details she was giving them, finding them too plausible, as though, particularly in the domestic elements of her life, she was relying on the truth.

After that everything she did, whether it was to repeat them exactly as she had given them before, or seemingly to forget them and replace them with alternative facts, confirmed his suspicion. They brought things to an abrupt end and Hector demanded another attempt.

And now Charles had dispensed with this fictitious man.

The man had done his best, summoned his life greedily, desperately, his eyes ransacked the corners of the room for it, the outline of the door, the unplugged telephone that, even if it had been connected, would only have been to the man at the bar, who knew where things in the back room were heading, and to whom they had given money not to care.

The fictitious man had been plausible, flawed, godly, hard-working, entrenched in loneliness and unable to work his way from it. He had names, dates, and then he died, and it had meant nothing, and redeemed nothing about what they had done in the train, and nothing about

214

the woman and her children, who seemed tediously like they might have been actually her children, straightforwardly the reason for her pleas.

This job, that had started out so promisingly, with a neatly handwritten letter asking for a death, as polite a contract as was ever taken out on a life, so strange that it seemed the trip might accrue strangeness, might be blessed with interest—but here they were, slaughtering ghosts and bored with it.

'We'll get some sleep,' says Hector. 'We'll get some sleep and then tomorrow we'll finish this job and maybe it will provide some interest, and either way we'll be done.'

'We'll get rid of this,' says Charles, gesturing to the body, 'we'll get some sleep, and then tomorrow we'll have our wits about us. We'll be able to take from this nuthouse whatever there is to be taken, and either way.'

'Either way we'll be done.'

PART 5

Years later, a phone call.

It wakes me, and at first I take the confusion to be mine, my tiredness keeping me at arm's length from sense. Then I recognise the voice and tell it to calm down, go slow. But the words come in gusts, and every one sounds cracked, broken over a knee before it's sent down the line.

This much I can figure: something deeply bad is with him at the far end of the call, it has shattered him and his language, and he wants me there.

I press words back into the rush, like, Wait and Slower, but I am pushing a tack into a wall while it falls onto me. Finally I get from the crackle of his broken words where he is, and I go to him.

I get there second to the police. Two of them: I push at the open door and as it creaks wide they turn to me and touch their holsters. I raise my hands obligingly. They have been standing over him. He is sitting on a footstool so small, so insufficient for the job, that it might be funny if it wasn't for his grin.

'What do you want?' The younger policeman, cheeks like scoops of ice cream. 'Go back downstairs.'

I tell them that he called me. They relax slightly without

taking their hands away from their guns.

'Called you when?' says the older one. Black hair, face like a claw hammer.

I shrug, and say thirty minutes, maybe forty.

'Take a seat there and use those big hands to keep your knees warm,' says claw hammer. 'Nothing in your pockets is worth getting shot for.'

I sit facing the grin—the chair sagging under me until we are almost as low as each other. Everything human in his eyes seems to have left. If he was in pieces when he called me then he has been put back together wrong, with a smile that isn't his.

'You got any other explanation you want to give for the noise?' the older button asks him. 'Any good enough we shouldn't take you in?'

'Make a stop on the way to wipe that look off your face,' says scoops of ice cream, raising an unconvincing fist.

Then from somewhere behind the grin he speaks, and his words aren't air-filled and broken any more. He says, 'I hope you're liking this.'

'What's that?' says the younger button, his cheeks turned cherry pink.

'I said I hope you're enjoying this, because you're on this case for one more second,' he says. 'As soon as you see what's behind that door it gets too big for you and you're back on the benches.' He has looked towards the bedroom door, closed tight, and the two police follow his look, the younger trying to play a smirk but scared. They draw their guns.

When they open the door, when they see what is in there, they swing their guns around like the walls are under arrest, like the air is under arrest. They shout at us to get on the floor, to get down on the floor and keep our hands up, keep our hands in sight, and I get on the floor, though every lick I've ever taken is telling me to do anything else, even if it's jump through the window, anything other than be restrained, be kept here with things gone as wrong as they've gone behind that door.

And he gets down on the ground too, the broken grin still on his face, his face inches from mine, like looking into a mirror, and I watch as the cuffs go on him and feel the metal tighten round my own wrists.

Then, in the end, after a lot of talking between themselves, months of talking about me over the top of my head, they bring me here.

————

Polly grows used on her visits to being questioned by young men in uniforms. They don't understand her reasons for visiting, and have been educated to know that if something does not make sense to them the failure can't be theirs but must belong to the old woman: she must, in fact, not understand her reasons for visiting. There must be some foolishness in her. (Maybe there *is* some foolishness in me, she thinks, to come here.) She is confused, and in need of a firm, kindly hand to send her safely home. Every time she arrives, she finds herself passed around a new pack of young men in white smocks, having to account for herself to each of them in turn—each slightly more senior than the last, none of them older or wiser than a fresh pot of white paint.

Until once she happens to visit on a Sunday, and she finds them responding to her differently, deferentially, with greater courtesy and fewer questions. They smile and nod and couldn't be much sweeter if she was carrying a police badge. From that day on she always wears a church hat to visit. That is all it takes to impress these unimpressive men, a church hat and a smart skirt, that is how simple these young men in smocks are. Now instead of wasting her time asking her why she wants to see such a danger-ous man, and telling her not to be fooled by the way he looks, instead of all that, they just ask if she knows where she is going. And more: they offer coffee, they ask if she needs help with her bag. All for wearing the right hat. So, fine—she dresses up like a respectable old lady and says *oh, thimbles* when she drops her pencil, if that's what it takes to be left alone.

Some of the young men she has even started to recognise one from the other, though they all wear the same bad haircut. Some have taken to calling her Mother, which they mean as a kindness, though who could wish for such sons?

Others come and go from one week to the next. Maybe, she thinks, they have found themselves not cut out for the work; maybe they've been intimidated by the occupants of this evenly lit and colour-coded dungeon which she dresses up nicely to visit.

She sees one of them quit. He is a bearded man, but otherwise she could hardly tell him from the rest. He is standing beside the door of a toilet, waiting for the reappearance of the inmate he has accompanied there. Except when the inmate emerges he is naked and covered in his own filth. The bearded man responds by removing his own smock as if he is planning to join in the nudity, but instead calls to a colleague and hands him the smock, renounces the job in vivid language, his face crimson under the beard, and walks for the exit. He has never been a parent, Polly guesses, so afraid of a little dirt. His ex-colleague trots after the naked, filth-covered man.

Today she smiles in what she hopes to be a church-like and motherly way and the boy stationed at the entrance smiles indulgently back. She makes her way through the green corridors into the blue and then red, passing him again, the same boy, in the same white smock, a half-dozen times more, the only difference whether he wears glasses and if he simpers or frowns.

The door at the corner is open. Inside he sits in the same spot, always. He sits by the window, looking out or seeming to. He is stained in ochre and sweat: his vest, his thin

trousers, his feet and neck. On his head there is the thing—
the mess of wood and pipework, like a cage, his hair and
beard growing wild around it.

He is completely still, perfectly ridiculous. He looks like
an old bear, dead in a trap.

She goes in the room and he turns to her, like he always
turns to her, like he always turns to anyone who puts a toe
across the invisible line that keeps his madness in this room
from all of the madness in all of the adjacent rooms, in these
red and blue and green and yellow halls, his eyes lighting
up with eagerness. 'Morning, Box,' she says, as his look
fades to nothing and he turns back to the window. Outside
on the ledge is a round little bird on matchstick legs.

Polly sits where she can watch Box watching nothing,
and from her bag she takes a newspaper and begins the
crossword.

————

I sit and think, which is all that is required of me, which
is plenty, to think and to wait until word comes, which it
will. I think with a kind of drifting contemplation, a slow
thinking, slow and charged. Thought hisses out of me, thin
as a gas, so they can't even see it as they edge around the
corners of the room or swim up through it and tip milk
into my mouth or stick me with needles and speak about
me like I'm absent, saying how I might be dead and who
would know.

I go breaking hands with _____ in memory, and ride the rollercoasters. We sit next to frying onions and we throw cards into a hat. We trail between corpses for Swagger and we go drinking with Swagger. A drifting contemplation. I go to see Evvie Heydt, and sit with her. I fall asleep with her beside me, and she wakes me. 'Hello there, happy bear.' Welcome thoughts of Evvie fill me, they crowd out everything and make sense of where I should be. I know what it is to be still and content. I go back to Evvie's, and go back again.

Be careful, some thinking is too much, is too hot and quick, and what is needed is a slow, drifting contemplation.

There is movement in the room, but it's nothing—Polly is taking her spot, putting down her bag, big as an automobile, getting out her newspaper.

I wonder if the skin beneath the strap, which once boiled purple and blistered and itched insufferably, has died, if my top few inches are already dead. If what I am waiting for, one of the things I am waiting for, is for the rest of myself to catch up.

Drift back into thought, into slow-punctured memories.

The apartment manager comes back and Lydia keeps him at a distance until she doesn't any more. She's pregnant. They're sitting on the steps counting cars with their son. Drift backwards. Lydia is pregnant, then she isn't and her husband is still run off and no one knows where. Childs is Swagger's gunsel, and _____ hasn't yet run out in the street and raised his head at the sound of the fair-ground and taken two shots in the back. We fall from the window of a hotel room, where a corpse has taken two shots at us and burned itself up, my hand is cut, and I try to tell _____ that Swagger is making us for the frame. Holcomb is dead, and he has a metal ball that can see the future and I plant it in the head of a crying man who has come to kill him. We bounce Gabriel off the walls and hide behind a hotel curtain and I am smoking a cigarette and patting the ash when _____ is thrown at my feet. _____ looks up at me. Like I am lying in his gutter.

More movement. A white smock. Come to pat at me and make notes on a clipboard and chew gum.

Drift into thought. Think about Cain and his ear. Think about going to Jarecki's after _____ has taken two in the back. Think about carrying a hotel drunk out into the street. This thinned-out thought, prolong it, this gas hissing out from me flooding the room and the device, giving the charge to the device, and all I need to do is sit and think and wait for word.

Of course once something terrible has been done it can't be easily undone, but it will be undone, with time. And all that is required of me is to think, which is a lot, which is plenty, and to wait.

Think about the apartment manager coming home and playing poker. Think carefully and prolong it. The apartment manager comes back and we are playing poker in the apartment that used to be _____'s and is now mine.

Lydia is watching the game but is mainly watching her husband, who has reappeared one day without explanation. Which is, I assume, the absolute best explanation he can give for the time he has been away. Specifics will do nothing to help his cause, which seems to be a sincere one: instead he comes back without them, ready to take his licks.

Except, he says (later he says this) there are no screams and no punches. Lydia stays in her bed, where she has shrunken into the sheets. His reappearance doesn't move her any further than onto her elbows. She lights a cigarette and holds it while he apologises and begs and explains the ways he has changed and some of the reasons, and she doesn't so much as move the cigarette to her lips, it just burns its way down to her knuckles. She asks him if he means it this time because she can't take it, can't take it not even once more.

'First time I ever knew I could hurt her,' he says.

Then a week where no one sees them, except when the apartment manager leaves to buy food and more cigarettes. They stay in their apartment and I imagine them like two dogs padding around each other in the street, uncertain, deciding if they're interested in fighting, or if they can get along.

It's a long time before Lydia eats a full meal or tells a joke, or lets her husband finish one of her stories or share her bed. 'For a long time,' he says, 'she wouldn't let herself cry when she looked at me, then she started crying and wouldn't stop. And still getting thinner, so thin you couldn't believe it. Anything I brought her she wouldn't eat—not hamburger, not buttered toast. She lived on cigarettes and nothing else.'

At some point they stop eyeing each other warily but they don't stop locking eyes, and she lets him back in her bed and then she is pregnant.

And all of the worry leaves her and goes into him. She stops looking at him like she's expecting the day when he will disappear again. She grows merry all round and rounds in the middle, and the apartment manager worries because she's old to be going through all being pregnant puts a woman through, and thin too. He lifts her feet for her and puts them on stools and brings her food, and now she eats it, with the calm of an endless field of cattle all comfortably doped.

I give him the cash for the rent and ask how she is and he smiles weakly and says, 'She's never been happier. I think my chest might be about to cave in though. I woke up today to blood on my pillow: turns out I've been gnawing on my hands.' He shows his right hand and every finger wears a bandage like a hat.

But when their son comes it is without incident. Does someone tell me she is serene throughout? Maybe I just imagine her as serene because now she is become serene, is always. To think of her any other way is to look at a lake and think it might boil.

I go back to Evvie's to tell her all this, how Lydia has forgiven the apartment manager, how serene she has become. Evvie has added another chain to her door and she keeps both of them across her. The door and the chains and the look she gives are all to keep me from her. 'Why are you still coming here, Box?' she says. 'What can I say that would get you to stop?'

———

'Take care, Mother,' says one of the boys cheerily as he leaves the room, and Polly smiles sweetly back. It must be nice, she thinks, to have no brain in your head.

'They condescend,' she says to Box. 'They think you are born at 100 and all set to die any day at 101, and in these last days of your dotage you must be grateful for any word or glance. A thought from an actual strong and living young man, oh dear oh my aged heart, the sweetest act of charity!' She fans herself dramatically with her newspaper.

She puts down the paper, bored with it. She has brought some knitting with her, or there is an apple in her bag too, which she could spend some time peeling and eating. She looks at Box as at a great undusted cabinet, tiring just by its presence.

As she sits in this empty room with this empty, absent man she'll find her mind thumbing its way through memories. Some of them she sits quietly with, some she speaks aloud.

Now something makes her think about Sue Gaston.

Some of this she says and some of this she only thinks, and it makes no difference what is said and what is only thought for all that reaches Box, sitting heavy in his own leaking thoughts:

When I was sixteen I had a boyfriend called Peter and Sue Gaston had a boyfriend called David, and we sat the two of them down and explained that we were swapping. Sue Gaston was my best friend at the time and died three years later when she was so bored by her parents' conversation that she tried to climb out of the window of their car, the first and only car that either of us had ever seen up close or been inside. The car was hardly moving—it was crawling the last few yards of the path to their house—but she slipped and fell with her head foremost, and the most Sue Gaston part of Sue Gaston went straight under a wheel and she popped like a porcupine, her fine legs still in the car, shoes kicking at the inside of her father's second greatest pride and joy, at that moment rolling itself to a promotion. My mother swore until her last day that she was standing at the sink doing the dishes and heard Sue's mother's scream when Sue popped, and that she knew it immediately for a mother's grief. Swore it even though we lived more than a mile away and I never but twice saw my mother do any dishes.

Anyway before she was nineteen and she popped like a porcupine, Sue Gaston was sixteen and she had a boyfriend called David, who she was bored with, and I had a boyfriend called Peter, who I thought I loved because I assumed that the first boy I kissed I would love forever.

I didn't realise how absolutely bored of Peter I was until Sue pointed it out to me, in the same way she diagnosed all my feelings for me when we were sixteen, the same way she had for years.

In my head I had built up a little married home with Peter that looked like my parents' home and like Sue's parents' home, and put in it a score of little boys who looked like Henry, Patrick and Anthony, my sweet little brothers, and one who looked like Christopher, my naughty little brother, and was naughty like him too. I would sit and daydream of being in my little home, like you're daydreaming now, Box, maybe, if that's what you're doing.

I would be pressing clothes or polishing everything in sight, and one of my good children would appear for a kiss on the cheek or the naughty child would appear with a torn jumper or a bruised eye and I'd smack him raw until he ran off crying to his room. Then Peter would come home from a day at the office, and I would take his troubles and his papers from him and help him off with his coat, and he would be just as much fourteen except that he would be wearing a moustache like Sue's father's moustache.

That was how it was in my head then. It was childish but it felt so much like my future and it very well might have been too.

So when Sue told me that I was bored with Peter I was very angry with her, because it felt as if she had reached into the space between my ears and knocked down the little house which stood there and flicked away the whole rest of my life. But she was right. It annoyed all heck out of me to find it out, if you'll excuse my language, but I couldn't deny that I was bored with Peter.

She told me that even as *she* had been growing bored of *David*, she had been thinking how well the two of us would get on together, and if I liked the idea of it then I should take him from her as a boyfriend until at least the summer, when her cousin was visiting, who was a better prospect for me all together. And by the summer, she said, I would be better at kissing because I would have had David as well as Peter to practise on.

You have to understand, Box, opportunities to pick and choose your pleasure were absolutely not for everyone in those days. They're still not, I'm sure, but back then they were particularly carefully managed. There are people who don't feel they can enjoy themselves if they're not keeping a close eye on how other people are enjoying themselves, and those people like to put themselves in charge of the world. Picking and choosing your pleasures and your lives certainly wasn't for decent young ladies like us. We were a pleasure for someone else, made to be chosen or not chosen and that was about the limit of it. Only try to tell Sue that. She was always someone who assumed her own freedom, that was just how she came in. And I was lucky enough to know her and she would take the time to talk me into believing in mine.

So when she told me that I was bored of Peter, if to begin with I couldn't see past the debris of the little marriage house in my mind and all the years of life swept away with it, it didn't take long before I began to remember that I had liked David before I liked Peter, and that he was cleverer at school and also a little more handsome. Sue said that she had seen Peter looking at her legs (we both knew they were particularly good legs) and that in her experience David was inclined to go along with anything, so we should just sit them down and explain to them that we were swapping. And that's what we did.

She was right that David seemed willing to go along with anything, but Peter spat teeth to begin with oh yes, and called both of us terrible names too, not quite under his breath. She just let him keep at it until he had begun to run out of words for us, and then told him that he could keep calling us any name he wanted but never speak to either of us again, or he could keep them to himself and be her boyfriend. Next day he was walking down the street holding her hand. By the end of the month, though, she'd got bored of him too, and that was that.

Three years later, when my best friend fell under the wheels of her father's car and popped, I felt very lost. I spent a summer checking for her in my purse. I saw her haunting me in mirrors like she'd become a cheap ghost as a joke.

It wasn't until after I'd had Evvie—to tell the truth, Box, it wasn't until I'd raised her, and she had gone off into the world and was making her own way with so much grace and determination—that I realised how much of my friend I had been carrying with me all those years, because I saw that I'd passed so much of her to my daughter.

She takes the apple from her bag and with it a small, sharp knife. Polly peels the apple, watching Box propped at his window. She looks at the strangeness of the device, the stains on his clothes, the armholes in his shirt sagging so badly she can see the chest within: the curve of flesh like a nippled nose, his drooping breast.

————

Think back to Lydia and the apartment, in slow, calm leaking thought.

Their son comes without incident and Lydia is serene throughout, or I imagine her as serene throughout, and their love for their son comes to them so easily, as if they were built for the task. Both can wrap their baby boy in cloth like it's a card trick, and then once he's dirtied it, both are ready to clean, boil and dry his wrapping—both are always feeding or entertaining him, they sit on the steps outside, counting cars together, pointing out colours to him, their love grows with him. It is something to see. It grows over the top of his head, and spills down onto him. He is a boy raised in a continual showering of excess love.

I sit in the dead apartment that _____ left when he died. I'm not in the fold of anyone else's intentions, not any more. I'm alone in my thoughts and I pickle in them.

There's no _____ to pull on any yoke with me because I gave him to Swagger, and no Swagger comes to shove me from corpse to corpse, or chase me out into the street and shoot me in the back. There's only Evvie, and as long as she won't see me or see sense there's no sense anywhere. I sit in that empty room in that dead apartment for so long I empty, until I'm nothing but limbs I don't recognise. I try to lift an arm or curl a toe, and the movement comes, but only at the far end of a long commute. I sit longer and I feel myself sever completely from the body in the chair.

My mind flails for something to be and with a cold horror that cuts through me tooth to tail, I find I'm Holcomb's Time Traveller and I sit in my machine with my mind cut loose and my body frozen in place. Thrash free and I'm the red triplets, that spin round each other, then round and into each other and separate out and I hang dislocated across these bodies, and to be in all of them means not to be in any of them and the fear cuts deeper, and my mind revolts again, and I'm still, seated. Not the Time Traveller but the fat clockmaker, every shadow in the room stabbing towards me, terrified out of any hope of movement, because I know what everyone knows: that every sharp edge, from a knife's blade to the ragged edge of a tin can, has in it a desire for the throat, and worse—that your own throat has its sympathy for every sharp edge.

I wake into myself. I wake into myself wondering what _____ was shot for, whether Swagger got anything for it, and plenty other things. What do I know about Lowden? I know how his face looks with the air squeezed from it. What do I know about Cansel? I know how his eyes widened as he escaped his burning sheet. As _____ drove his knife into his face, how he screamed. I need to get some control, before I lose it all again, and I go to Holcomb's apartment to look for it.

I go to Holcomb's, where they wrung the life from him and it's as if time died in here with him: the writer's not here (not even as a stain on the bed: the mattress is gone) but everything else is like it was when _____ and I went through it, after we'd found him, eye ready to drop from his face, a hole in his cheek.

There is still no copper ball that can hold the future and the past.

But I take his handwritten notebooks and his typewritten pages, and all the hundreds of thousands of words he'd sold off one by one to the pulps. I find them in magazines he had in drawers, in magazines under his bed, in a magazine levelling his kitchen table. They are under the name Holcomb, and also some, in older magazines, under a different name, Campbell, though the writing is recognisably Holcomb's and fragments in the notebooks mark the stories as his.

It takes me a long time reading Holcomb's stories and notebooks to learn how to read them. Each time through, more of them is available. I get to know Holcomb's handwriting until the two of us are so familiar that I can follow it even when it's drunk out of its skull. I begin to see in the different machines and scientists and ways of describing time what will be useful and how to discard the rest.

In one slurring, drunk-sliding passage of a notebook I find something about a time traveller who discovers that time isn't a single line—past at one end, future at the other, us pushed along its length—but something multiplying, branching:

> NOT flowing, but RIGID. The past and future are as real and fixed as the present, but they exist in infinite variety. Every branch of time, and they are INFINITE, represents a possible other creation, each one different from the others by one single degree. Across the sum of them all exists everything in every possible variety.

So everything that didn't happen here, happened there, or it happened one branch further across, and every sorry act that is committed over here, somewhere it isn't. Crawl far enough back up the branches, then you could get one to the other. You could move out of your version of things and into any other: your pick.

The next passage arrives like a hangover. It's about Holcomb not his scientist—all his writing works back to self-pity. This passage ends: *I'm writing this and yesterday I did and didn't shoot myself.*

*

Holcomb's versions of time, his different machines: they talk against each other, Holcomb and Campbell disagree constantly with each other and with themselves. They put together models of the universe and they bury them in scrubland, and make more. I pick through it all to find what's useful, and I begin to see in the notes and the dropped half-details of some of the stories the outline of the device.

Drift in thought. Evvie is kind to me and takes my hand, and I fall asleep in her apartment and when she wakes me, it is softly. 'Hello there, happy bear.' I spend the night at the New Europe, and I don't think for days about where _____ is, maybe because I know.

I go back to Evvie's. Only she sends me away. As if I didn't sleep in her apartment, as if she didn't wake me softly, and tap on my tooth, and kiss me, and bandage my hand. This, she says, was pity or kindness. She says that she was decent to me because I came to her, but it doesn't give me a right over her, not to keep coming, not to insist she feel some way she doesn't, and all the pity and kindness is in the past and none of it is to be repeated.

She should know how easy love is if it's just freely given, how it multiplies from itself: I've seen it in Lydia and the apartment manager and how they are with their son, it will grow and grow if she just lets it. I'm frustrated and I let her feel some of my frustration. She is acting as if she didn't open the door to me and, seeing me there, with a cut hand, covered in dirt from paying off a debt, *her* debt, because hadn't it travelled on to her?—as if I wasn't entitled to something.

She talks to me like you'd talk to an unwelcome stranger, like you'd talk to someone you were wary of. She keeps her door between us. As if she could hold me off if I chose to press myself, if I chose to explore into her room, to find with my hands what it is I'm entitled to. She asks me what it is I want, as if she hadn't shared the ease and contentment of our sitting together, as if she hadn't put her hand in mine.

I know I can make a life around Evvie Heydt, I can keep at her, I can crawl through possibilities until I do.

———

Polly is reading her newspaper and one of the men in white smocks interrupts her. He has been spinning a powder round in a container of milk, dissolving it. 'Would you mind?' he says and holds the milk out to her. He wants her to do his work for him, to stand by Box, reach into the frame of the device and part the damaged lips, to tip the milk into his mouth. To nurse him.

'No,' she says, with a voice to crack chinaware, 'I'm not doing that.' She feels like she might punch the young man in the nose. He frowns, and begins the job himself. Polly finds herself too full of anger for the young man to go back to the paper. She watches him instead.

When he is finished he leaves the room. Polly pulls her

chair closer to Box and looks through the mesh of the device into his eyes, though she doesn't find him there.

'I hate you,' she says, though the tone of her voice is friendly. She pats him on the leg with her rolled up newspaper. 'I hate you so much it hurts me to be in here with you. Maybe that's why you wear all of this,' she says. 'This treehouse you've built yourself into. To stop me coming at you with a knife. Well, I won't. You're not the first son of a bitch I've known.'

Polly thinks back to the reporter who visited her here. One of the attendants must have known someone, perhaps they were even paid for the tip.

She arrived one day and there, already in her chair, was the man—young, scrawny, with a sharp nose and dark, thick, back-combed hair. The chair itself was closer to the window than it would usually be, and the window was open wide. The man had a phoney smile that slid into place when Polly came in the room. He bounced up and offered her the seat with an expansive gesture. He didn't introduce himself but, as she sat, stood a few paces behind her, hands clasped behind his back, looking thoughtfully at Box and refusing to catch her eye, as if this was a show they had arranged to meet at.

Irritated, she ignored him, and was deciding if she could do it better by reading the sleek she had in her bag, when, without altering his gaze, he said, 'This must be a very emotional experience for you.'

She chewed on her teeth. He stood a while longer and then tried, 'It's hard to say how brave you are to come here.'

Rather than say anything, she chose to be every bit as still and empty as Box. She'd tire this man out by not responding. She wouldn't reward him for surprising her— trapping her with his presence.

It didn't take long: a few minutes, a few more unanswered comments, and he started to fidget where he stood. Then he coughed twice into his hand. At that, a photographer appeared in the open window and popped a bulb at her, and both of them were gone.

Polly saw the story when it ran. The picture of her in her big church hat, full of anger for the photographer, Box in his machine, full of nothing at all, and both looking as mad as each other on their folding chairs in this bare little room. It called her the Madhouse Mother, and had quotes from her that made her saintly and kind and were generally horseshit. It was from that article and the couple more it bred that some of the attendants took to calling her Mother. She read like a character in a story—this odd version of herself who spoke about how she forgave Box for what he had done.

She felt almost jealous of this other her.

'Maybe I should have forgiven you by now,' she says. 'I hoped I would, after all these months. I know you didn't pick your brain from a shelf, because none of us do, so I should be able to say: he was made this way, vicious and selfish, and then he was sent out on a path to kill my daughter. He didn't choose any of it, not his brain, not the path. I know that I'm a piece of meat in this skillet,' she says tapping her head, 'or else some God made me some way, and whichever it is I didn't get a say in what I was given. And if you're a nasty piece of spoiled meat I guess it wasn't your doing either.'

She says, 'Well, I'm going to keep sitting here in my skillet and thinking how you're stuck in yours, because I don't know what to do with hating you.' She opens her newspaper.

———

When they first bring me here, another man is sitting in the room with me. My sight is blurred, it often is, and I think maybe the other man is Bernard, but when I ask him he laughs and it isn't, though he is large like Bernard. He sits and talks with me for a while. He is saying how violence has momentum, once it arrives it leads on into itself, and that is the beautiful thing about it. How long do we spend just looking for the next thing to do, he asks, but violence can fill space, any space it is given, like sunlight filling a room, can surround you every inch like bathwater. And here we've been led into it, and maybe there are worse places to be, and I feel quite afraid of him, even though I understand exactly what he means.

*

I build the device so quickly it is as if I'm already guided, as if unseen practice has already taken me to it. I know that I don't have to make a great machine the size of a car that can be climbed into. It is going to be a device that sits around my head, with two straps that I make from a belt to hold it in place: one running from the crown under the chin, the other from the forehead to the back of the neck.

The device is simple because it has to do something simple. This is one of the clearest things I take from Holcomb's writing, that manipulation of time is a cinch, however much we struggle to think it. Even crossing a room is hard until you learn to walk. To step back through time is no harder. I pull the mirror from the wall in the bathroom of the dead apartment, and I go to Lydia's and I take two large mirrors from her, and I sit the mirrors around the table as if the four of us are going to play a friendly game of cards. I take apart the headboard of the bed and use the wood to build a brace that sits across my shoulders, which holds the pieces of device in place as I build it around my head, using the mirrors to watch myself work. All the device requires is a frame of pipes that are braced against important points of the head, close to the leaking thoughts that power and guide its use, and the pipes find their home easy and quick. The device has a sharp edge across the top of my skull and I bleed into my hair without noticing, then I pad the edge and adjust the pressure of the nails that top the pipes to give the device claws to hold itself against me as it needs to, and I unbuild the brace from my shoulders and it perches there, complete and perfect. And I sit in drifting contemplation, slow leaking thought, and the feeling is as if the grip of the machine is taking each quarter of my head and turning it out from the rest, and machine and head ladder out into the apartment and in every direction at once. I climb through the cracked space.

I drift in contemplation and find myself outside Holcomb's. It's night time, the rain is coming down, and the street is empty, but the phone booth is dark and by it lies a heap, a dark mass. I step towards it as I appear in the doorway of the building alongside _____, and I see Swagger lying there, half in, half out of the booth, his gun steadying on us, and in the doorway I have reached down and I throw a rock, and Swagger's gun fires twice but he's missed his shot, and I see myself dive backwards into the building onto _____. I take to my heels as Swagger takes to his heels.

I drift further and I am in the apartment, and _____ is here, and Swagger too and Childs, and I interrupt their preparations. I interrupt their preparations. It is still _____'s apartment and not yet mine. They are sitting at _____'s table with their sleeves rolled up high, their fingers tipped oil-black: Swagger, Childs and _____. I am off at Evvie's apartment, but I am here too, and I have a chance to keep _____ from being shot in the street. My hand is cut from the fall from Cansel's window. Lying before the three of them on the table and reflected in their eyes are barrels, chambers, firing rods, ammunition—the guts and grease of guns, maybe half a dozen guns, maybe more.

Swagger is holding a chamber, a black glistening beetle that he has run through with a long brush, piercing one of its five eyes. Childs' hand is turning and polishing a trigger guard with a cloth. Between them _____ is holding a shotgun stock. He is looking at the spread laid out before him on a sheet like a picnic, looking greedily, like he can't wait to take these guts in his guts, like he'll eat them up until he is lead-bodied, until he can spit bullets wherever Swagger points him.

'Take a seat, Box,' says Swagger. 'We're getting ready. Things are about to break.'

I don't take a seat but I don't find any words for him, or for _____.

Childs stands. He takes a Colt Super Match from the table and walks over to me. His hoofed leg is a corked gun barrel. He is holding the Colt backwards, shaking hands with the barrel, and he knocks its handle against the back of my cut hand. I keep my arms by my side. Childs' breath steams upward into my face. 'Take the gun,' he says, and raps my hand with it again. He strikes downwards, the inside of the butt against my knuckles, scraping them. My fist clenches and I feel the palm open with blood. The stub of Childs' missing arm rises up, aroused, like it wants to grip me by the neck. The gun's handle swipes my hand again.

'Things are about to break,' says Swagger. I look at _____. 'We're going to go calling on a friend of Lowden's, a friend of Lowden and Cansel—Dickie's his name. We're going to be ready. Things are about to break. Take a seat, Box.'

'_____,' I manage to say, 'let's go.'

Already he is up, standing beside Childs. No one moves like _____. He takes the gun from the cripple, who backs off.

_____ cradles the gun in his hands and when he speaks he speaks to the gun.

When _____ spoke—when he wasn't screaming or threatening death or cursing and spitting teeth, when he was just talking—he always sounded like a boy.

'Box,' he says, 'there's Dickie, and we're going to go pay him a visit. Things are about to break.'

I don't know what to say. We've been pulling at the same yoke for so long I don't know how to move without him moving too. 'They j u st want—They'll cop you.' Isn't this enough to say?

Swagger is always his own fanfare. He is in a vest but still has on his hat. I can't look at him. 'Because of the fire? Is that what this is?' he asks. 'That you burned Cansel?' He runs his thumbs the height of his suspenders and lets them snap against his chest, then rubs and slaps at his belly like it's the family dog. 'Don't worry about that. That was just some quick thinking, on your part. Cansel's dead,' he says. 'The rest is just colour.'

He walks so close to me we are both sharing his hat's brim.

'There's one more job for you boys. One more job to get

this whole thing tied up, so take a seat, Box.'

I take myself out from under Swagger's hat, but I can't manage any more words. I look at _____ and hold out my cut hand to him. I think maybe he'll take the hand— maybe just to hurt the cut he'll take the hand, to punish me for the gesture.

He looks greedily into his gun. I make for the door.

When they leave I follow them all the way to the fence, Dickie, who takes them into his office building which is as threadbare and old as he is, with his long, thin hair and elbow patches. I wait around the back of the building, where I can see the fire escape. I hear one shot and see the flash, two storeys up. Then I see _____ at the window. He has a gun in his hand, and raises it at Swagger, or Childs, and pulls on the trigger. But of course his gun, the gun they've given him, does nothing. _____ comes through the window, and shots come with him. He must have taken one in the arm because he clutches it as he passes me, blood in his fingers. I've put myself in the dark where he can't see me, I follow in the shadows, behind Swagger, who's after him. At the corner, _____ stops. He drops the gelded gun and stands in the street with his head raised as if he's sniffing. He's listening. From all the way at the fairground there's sound carried by the wind. He hears the band organ, and the screams from the double chutes and the Human Roulette Wheel, and he turns as if he thinks that the best way to run, and Swagger takes his shot.

I leave: I'll leave _____ and go to Evvie. But I'll come

back. This is just a rehearsal. First I'll make things right with Evvie, I'll take Evvie, and I can get it so _____ doesn't end up on a street corner with a gelded gun sniffing at air.

There's some neck pain, from holding the device. But then there's some back pain from sitting too, and there's probably some pain that comes from having shoulders and wrist pain from having wrists. Everything a person has comes to pain them. It's another thing to carry, this pain, like the device, but it's not more to carry than I can bear. Why would it be easy, why should it be quick? I sit in the device and think with my attention diffused, just like Holcomb calls it: a state of drifting contemplation.

———

The first time Polly came here, after four or five men in white smocks had passed her around and each one of them had tried to talk her out of seeing the man she'd come to see, and then the final two had warned her about how strange he would look when she saw him, she still found herself shocked. She stood in the doorway a full minute, while the attendant who had brought her checked his watch and rocked on his heels.

The instant she put a foot into the room, when Box, who had been so still he could have been taxidermy, turned to look at her, it could have scared her blood out from under her skin. Then he just turned back to his window and his stillness.

She spoke to the attendant about the thing around Box's head. 'We don't like to have him in it,' said the attendant, abashed, as if he has been caught spoiling this dangerous, guilty man like a pet, 'but when they took it from him he was very violent. This way we don't have any trouble from him.'

Now she sits and eats a carrot. Over the course of the day she has finished a crossword, and knitted, and bored of knitting, and she has eaten half a dozen carrots. They are big, crisp, sweet carrots that a friend brought her from her garden. She'll reach into her bag—the bag large enough to set to sea in—take a carrot from it, bite off the end and spit it back into the open bag. Then she'll sit and thoughtfully chew through the rest of the carrot. When she finishes it she gives a big sigh about nothing in particular. 'You're not the first son of a bitch I've known,' she says towards Box.

She once knew a son of a bitch who got a bottle buried in his head in a bar fight. She knew everyone who drank at that bar—everyone who drank there knew everyone who drank there—and she was there when the fight broke out and saw the bottle come down on the head of this son of a bitch, and a shard the width of a hand that went through the top of his skull, straight down. Polly taps her head with two fingers to show. And it stayed there as if it had been set on a table. 'I just about fell clean out of myself when I saw it,' she says.

The son of a bitch sat on the ground blinking, feeling around the bottle like he was trying to find a light switch. They took him to the hospital like that, and he walked with them, the bottle still there. He had to bend his knees to get through the door because of the extra height of the bottle.

After that day he became good-tempered, charitable as a nun. His wife left, said she couldn't recognise him any more, and that he kept giving away all their money, to anyone. 'That's how deep that piece of glass cut him,' Polly says. 'It was like a word had been crossed out on a sheet of paper, and everything he'd ever been with it. The son of a bitch just got cut away and left someone else.'

'Chester was a son of a bitch too, of course,' she says. 'Plenty would tell you.'

She thinks about when she and Chester became engaged, and the engagement became known, and she started to get letters. They came from family members and friends, and more than one came without any name on it, and all warning about him. They told her all the things they knew Chester had done and many more they'd heard he might have. 'People who hadn't said two words to me in years decided that they had to warn me of the sort of man I was marrying, and they sat down and wrote me long letters,' she says. 'They let me know he'd been to jail, and more, and you could feel that they loved writing those letters.'

She thinks through all the things they wrote. Reading the letters didn't make her angry. Certainly, there was nothing in them to surprise her much. It hadn't been long since she had met Chester, but they'd always talked: to the exclusion of everything and everybody else, they talked, from the day they met. She knew the man she was going to marry, and knew the man he had been. Still the letters frightened Chester. He worried they would work. He tried to move forward the date of their wedding. It was that which got her angry. 'I told him—thimbles to that. Though not in those words. As if I'd change my wedding plans by as much as a single day because of those cowards. Ha,' she says. She would not be deterred from the wedding by any letter writer; she would not be made to speed it up by Chester. They got married the day they'd always intended to. Two of her brothers didn't come and she never spoke to them again.

'It never occurred to any of them—the disapprovers, the letter-writers—that there might be stories about me too, of course,' she tells Box. 'They were incapable of thinking that a person might have more than one life, might be more than a half-inch deep.'

She stands and stretches out her back. It's tiring, spending days sitting in this empty room. She walks two circuits around Box and then peers into the gridded face. She examines the tangle of hair, the beard overgrowing its trellis.

Box's eyes don't follow her. That scaffold around his head, just an empty Box within a box within a box.

She says, 'I liked you, Box, the first time we met. For nearly half an hour I liked you. That's how slow I am at thinking, how wrong I can be.' She takes her seat again.

She thinks back to that time, the one time she met Box before Evvie's death, before Box scurried out of his mind—or sank deep into it—and became just taxidermy here, in this eerie place.

It was a Sunday and she was roasting a lamb and waiting for Evvie, who was going to come and have dinner with her. There was a knock on the door, earlier than Polly expected, and when she opened her door it wasn't Evvie she found there but this tremendous man, so big that the first thing she did was laugh out loud at the size of him, and then she couldn't help but laugh again at her own rudeness when she saw him blush at it. He had his hat bunched up in his hands like he was nervous, and when she got his name from him in a couple of struggling, breathy sentences that just endeared him more to her, and she thought she had him pegged: a sweet lunk, the sort of troubled soul Evvie picked up without even trying, brought them to her just by moving about the world. Polly assumed that her daughter had invited this man to join them for dinner, and so she brought him in, gladly. She sat him down at her kitchen table and said, 'Well, it'd be a crime to waste a grip like you must have on you,' and set him to squeezing lemons, and they worked together: Box squeezing lemons for lemonade, Polly sugaring and watering, and checking the lamb, and wondering if she had any furniture that she needed moving or cars she wanted thrown over the house, while she had this man who could reduce a lemon to dust in half a second.

They were listening to music on the radio and Polly was trying to win a dollar from Box with a card trick when, half an hour later, Evvie came through the door. Polly's laugh caught in her throat when she saw her daughter's face. She turned to Box whose eyes dived to the ground, his jaw pulled tight, his hands shook. Evvie shouted at Box. 'Why do you do this?' she shouted, and Polly couldn't think of the last time she'd heard Evvie shout. 'Is it just to frighten me? To show me that you can?'

Polly stood and told Box to leave in a voice that could have bent a tommy gun.

But Box just turned obstinate and silent. Polly could do nothing to move him. Evvie started spinning on the spot, her arms gripped tight around herself, it unnerved Polly to see her so shaken. Box was just a malicious silent growth, a mould that sulked on a kitchen chair. Evvie had been speaking to herself, but now she grabbed Polly with both her hands and whispered in her ear that she would go and call for someone, and that if Box left, if he followed her when she went, if he did anything at all, then she shouldn't try to stop him.

She went out the front door, and Box didn't follow. He

just sat silent, sullen in the chair. Soon she sat too. Her in her fresh hatred, Box in whatever dark mood kept him in his place.

'I liked you, Box, for nearly half an hour,' Polly says.

When the doorbell went again Polly found another man there, twice the size of a bridge, hat crushed in his hands. She wondered if her house was going to fill up with these gigantic men, and thought how it wouldn't take many. This one's nose was squint on his face, like a curtain pulled closed too sharply. He introduced himself as Bernard. He addressed himself to her politely and said that he'd been told that Box was here. He had come to get him.

Polly let him in and watched without knowing how to be in the presence of this strange scene, while Bernard spoke to Box, pressuring him gingerly, handling him as you do a tired child.

Soon Box, still without a word, stood, put on his hat and left. Bernard followed him, leaving gentle apologies like footmarks in a thick rug.

———

I sit in the device, I think slow, drifting thoughts, and I'm blinked in and out of existence, I'm cracked open, I crawl through the cracks, and I find myself outside Holcomb's again.

It's day and the glass in the phone booth is uncracked.

I go in and up the stairs and as I approach the open

door of the writer's apartment I hear the pecking of his typewriter, and expect to find him sitting at his desk, and maybe find myself sinking into his couch, reading his magazines or sleeping on duty.

Except it's Swagger that sits at the typewriter. Only he is taller than he can possibly be. If Swagger is half a foot taller than most men, now he is half a foot taller than himself, and the fit isn't right. He looks up and grins wide. I ask him what he is typing. He says he is typing up his official report on the Gold Mask Killers. He says that everyone knows the story of Mike Swagger and the Gold Mask Killers. I don't know the story, I say, and his smile and his size and his presence here in this place all make me dogsick. Sure you do, Box, but why don't I tell you some of it anyway. Take a seat, Swagger says. Swagger says:

One day I was in my office sitting carefully under my hat.

I had a hangover like a stampede round a bathtub and I'd just taken the bottle from my desk to nurse it when Marly opened the communicating door. She looked me up and down with that indulgent, scornful look she has. 'I'd say you looked like death,' she said, 'but I'm pretty sure I just met him.'

'That so?' I asked. 'I'd have been grateful if he'd made it here a couple of hours ago, but now I'm inclined to try and beat the rap.'

'It wouldn't be the first time,' she said, smiling. But then her expression changed to something serious. For a second she took my hand in her soft grip and told me to be careful. 'Whatever he wants, just be careful,' she said. 'I've got a bad feeling about this one.' Well, I ought to have wised up enough to listen to her feelings by now.

I tried to exude the well-mannered confidence of the modern private eye, and Marly showed in our visitor: one Mr Jean Cansel. She wasn't wrong—he looked like death, like a horror flick. He was made of great, long bones draped with thin skin. But it was the man's head . . . Most secretaries with this Cansel as their first customer of the day would have been found a week later, their hearts stopped, hair whitened, aged a hundred years in shock. He probably left a trail of them everywhere he went.

The horrifying Mr Cansel took a seat and we exchanged pleasantries. He told me that he was looking for a man by the name of Jack Campbell, though he thought Campbell might be calling himself something different. You knew him by a different name, didn't you, Box? He called himself Holcomb.

'Good friend of yours,' I asked Cansel, 'this man whose name you're not sure of?'

'I am quite aware, Mr Swagger,' said Cansel, 'that you are being flippant, but I hope you will not mind if I do not participate in your badinage.'

'Entirely fine, Mr Cansel,' I said. 'Badinage comes as part of the service, you won't be billed any extra for it,' and I took a cigar from the box I keep and chewed into it.

Cansel explained that he had never met Mr Campbell, but that he used to work for the man's family, as a 'retainer', he said, employed by Campbell's uncle. 'The family's wealth,' he said, 'unfortunately, dissipated and, although we might both have wished it otherwise, it became ne-ses-serry'—he split his words like this, and with an accent I found hard to place—'for us to part ways. I recently learned, with some not insubstan-ti-al sadness, that he had passed away. A final request from my old employer was passed on to me: that I find his nephew—Mr Jack Campbell—and inform him of his loss.'

He said that some small amount of money had been given him to find Campbell, and some small amount more was set to go to Campbell, the scant remains of the uncle's wealth. 'Where exactly is it you come from, Mr Cansel,' I asked. Cansel gave a smile that did not make him appear a hair's breadth less ghastly and not a shadow's weight more amused.

> *As Swagger performs the smile, his own great head takes on the skull of Cansel: his eyes are pitted, his cheekbones sharp.*
> *A new voice, coarse and sharp and strangely accented comes from him as he speaks for Cansel.*

'I have travelled, Mr Swagger,' Cansel said, but he wouldn't be moved from his subject. 'As well as Mr Campbell's name, I can provide you with this'—he handed across the desk a small photograph—'and tell you that he previously worked as a writer of stories for

257

magazines. How long do you think it will take you to locate him, Mr Swagger?'

The photograph showed a man in his 20s or early 30s, light-haired, well groomed, with a boyish handsomeness and a look on his face that seemed to suggest that he liked the photographer but felt tortured by what they were doing to him. 'He wrote for the sleeks?' I asked.

'I believe,' replied Cansel, 'that he wrote romantic stories. A pulp writer.'

That was about the end of the meeting with the ghoul. He laid out enough money to keep us working for the rest of the week, and told me he could be found at the Ambassador Hotel, then dusted, though if he'd gone through the window on great bat wings, I wouldn't have blinked.

Swagger is larger still.

The typewriter looks like a toy in front of him,
the desk looks like a miniature, a practical joke.

When Childs got to the office I told him the story. 'I wish you'd been here to talk Mike out of taking his money, Childs,' Marly said. Childs was taking off his artificial leg, having a preference for sitting without it. 'I haven't stopped shivering since that man walked in the door.'

I shrugged and said, 'No sense turning away good money because we didn't care for how its companion looked.' I told Childs to find this Campbell, and get a read on why someone might be looking for him. 'Then we can decide whether to feed him to the ghoul.'

Except Swagger met Holcomb.

It was at _____'s card table. He was there to collar a
salesman called Polk and I don't know how that squares
with this story which begins with the ghoul, Cansel.
It hurts my head that it doesn't square,
and I struggle to think while Swagger speaks,
while he shifts and swells.

Childs found Campbell easy enough. He had once collected a paycheque made out to his old name at a magazine, and that was all it took to match him to Holcomb.

So Childs went to pay this Holcomb or Campbell a visit.
Campbell seemed surprised to learn that he had an uncle
to lose: he practically shooed Childs out the door. I guess
he would have blown town, would have taken up another
new name and left behind a new string of debts.

Except the ghoul, or an associate of his, had trailed Childs.
They followed him all the way to Campbell's door—even
though trailing Childs is no mean job. And before we could
decide if we wanted to hand Campbell over—and before
Campbell could vanish himself—they got to him . . .

I took a call from the buttons that night. And I can't
describe to you the fury I felt looking down at that boy's
corpse. They'd taken their time with him, Cansel and
whoever he worked with. They'd had their fun. They'd
wrung his neck, and worse than that. Then the last thing
they did was put a bullet through his cheek.

I promised myself I was going to find them, the men
who had done this work. We had led them straight to their

victim, and I didn't plan to forget it.

Cromarty, head of the buttons, was there, and he tried to reassure me. 'There have been plenty of times that crooks have used an honest agency to do their dirty work for them,' he said, but it was no good. The night lit with my anger and my voice rose to a preacher's roar as I answered him—every flatfoot in that apartment turned to watch. 'Cansel and everyone who worked with him, they're all going to pay for this. They don't get to decide that this kid deserved to die!'

Swagger's mouth grows wider and wider, it is a hothouse and a loudspeaker, his words shake the room.

'They're going to be sorry for the day they turned Mike Swagger into a weapon, because it's not going to be cop justice they're going to get, it's not going to come to them through a jury, it's going to come from the barrel of a gun. And I'm going to make sure it isn't quick. They're going to feel it, and they're going to pray for it to be over.'

The first call I made when I left the site of the killing was to a love interest of Campbell's who Childs had made, a dame called Evelyn Heydt.

'Mr Swagger,' she said, 'I heard about your ghoul. I had every question you've just asked me from the police.'

She sounded abrupt and hurt and couldn't have known less about Campbell if she'd been studying not knowing about him for weeks. She had a real beauty, which she seemed to resent sharing. When she walked me out the door I felt evicted from warmth into the cold city. I walked to a drugstore and made a call to the office to see if Childs had left any messages.

I smoked a cigar and stomped my feet and couldn't shake the feeling that there was something I had missed, something I hadn't thought to ask, or hadn't wanted to, and it took me back to Evelyn Heydt's apartment.

When I got there, the vestibule door was open. Then I found the door to her apartment just slipping closed. I caught it, quietly, and I pressed my eye to the gap to peer in.

> *He squints at me, leans forward,*
> *his eye, jelly white, size of a fishbowl, peers.*
> *I could hang on his eyelashes like rope.*
> *I could punch straight through his pupil.*

What did I see there, Box?

I pressed my eye to the gap and I saw the backs of two men, the smaller of them carrying a knife. They were approaching Evelyn Heydt, who was retreating, beautiful and afraid.

CHRIST, I felt angry.

> *His fists crash down and the typewriter*
> *leaps from the desk.*

I've known men like this, who think they're tough because they can throw a scare into a frail. And I've known women who've been cut up, and worse, because some dirty crook was enjoying his own power too much to know when to quit. I gripped my Colt like I already had them by the neck, and eased my way into the room.

The smaller of the two men was speaking, his voice raspy and vicious. 'Box, why don't you tell her what we came for?' he said. Then the other one—you—started to speak. Only I swung the door shut and the noise made the two of you turn to the barrel of my Colt. To make sure you noticed it, I cocked the hammer. 'Why don't you tell me what you came here for,' I said, 'while the lady gets busy calling the police.'

Swagger tells me what happened at Evelyn's,
the words pressing against my memory of the scene as I
thought it went, overwhelming it.
He has grown until his back is bent against the ceiling.
His hands by the typewriter are as big as kitbags.

'Oh Mike!' Evelyn Heydt ran to me, keeping as much furniture between herself and her two intruders as she could. I could feel the squeeze of her body against mine, full of gratitude, and promise. 'Thank God, Mike! You made it here just in time,' she said.

'Always, sweetheart,' I said. 'Go and raise a couple of buzzers, while I ask these two who sent them crawling out their holes.'

When she was out of the apartment I used the long barrel of the Colt to invite you both to sit. Your friend with the knife sneered at me. 'You can stand or you can sit,' I said. 'However you like it. But I mean to get some answers out of you. We don't have a lot of time before the cops get here so I might not be able to ask nice. You two don't look like you've got a lot of smart ideas sparking in your heads, so I'm going to assume someone told you to come here. Who was that?'

Your friend with the knife swung his arm up, the knife disappearing into itself before he dropped it into his pocket. Then he spat at my feet.

I almost pulled the trigger then. 'You're quite the tough little _____, aren't you?' I said.

I wanted to put a hole in this little loogan's side. Even Cromarty wouldn't have given me a hard time about it, some vicious little torpedo who'd broken in to rasp threats, a scar across the side of his chin: no one would mind if they had to patch up a bullet hole before they put the cuffs on him. 'The only reason I haven't dropped you with a bullet,' I told him, 'is because she seems like a nice girl, and I don't want her to have to clear your blood out of her carpet.'

Then you took a half-step at me, remember, Box?

I try to remember visiting Evvie's that first time,
seeing her at her window, pressing our way into her
space, pursuit in slow steps,
her eyes big as spotlights, distress coiling in her throat,
a liquorice taste of new words forming in mine.
I remember it, but not as he tells it,
nothing squares, not even close. And the ceiling bends
across Swagger's back with each breath he takes.
He licks at his lips with a tongue like a wet towel.

And from the door came Evelyn's voice, and it was timid and fragile. 'Mike,' she said.

I stepped back as I turned so I could keep the gun on you, and there she was in the doorway, a snub-nosed automatic pressed against her temple. 'I trust it won't be nessess-ary to shoot Ms Heydt,' said the ghoul, Cansel, from behind the doorjamb, his long fingers tight around her upper arm.

He must have found her on the stairs. 'You killed Holcomb,' I said, 'and you're going to die for it.'

'I am not a murderer, Mr Swagger, and I hope you do not mean to turn me into one,' said Cansel.

That's how he got you out of there, you and your vicious little friend, by taking an innocent girl and pressing the barrel of a gun against her pretty head.

Cansel is a tall corpse we find under a bloody sheet in a hotel room, but somehow he is in Evvie's apartment with a gun pressed to her temple, somehow we work with him. Swagger is a private eye, he is wearing his vest, his holster, his gun—all of it is vast, he's an alleyway I'm trapped in, he's the buildings pressing all around.

At Cansel's instruction, I put my gun on the ground and let the two of you leave. I traded your sorry lives for hers, and you scurried off into the night, like vermin. Cansel followed you down the stairs, muscling Evelyn with him. I watched from the top of the landing, which was as far as he would tolerate me to come, as he shouted from the outer door, 'Goodbye, Mr Swagger. I hope very much never to see you again,' and went, leaving the girl. With Evelyn safe, I gave chase, but the ghoul had vanished.

I tell Swagger that my head hurts and
he laughs a colossal laugh.
I think of the cacophony of giants in Holcomb's story.

I'll skip some, then. Cansel went to Holcomb's girl maybe because there was something he needed to know or just to throw a scare into her and keep her quiet: either way, it didn't matter. He hadn't jumped town, and he wasn't safe, not from me.

You don't need to hear about Lowden—a fumbler in antiques, a rich amateur. We found him because Campbell had mentioned the name once to Evelyn Heydt. And you don't need to hear about Dickie, Lowden's sometime fence. Though it was Dickie who finally told us what the ghoul was chasing . . .

In a previous life, half a continent from here, Campbell had run up a lot of debt, and fled. He came to town, put on a new name like it was a change of clothes and maybe he thought he was safe. But our ghoul, Cansel, drew a bead on him, bought up the debt and chased him down.

Swagger has grown so big there is no space in the room
to stand, I'm pressed up against the wall. His tooth
swings open like a door and I go inside the hot cavern of
his mouth and his voice surrounds me.

Except the trail went cold on Cansel. To find his mark he had to come to my office.

We led him, along with some stray muscle he hired, straight to Campbell, and I don't plan on forgiving myself for it.

Cansel, or you and your friend, or all of you together, put Campbell through the wringer. You wanted to get as much of the debt out of him as you could.

Except Campbell had spent all his money on leg shows and drink. He couldn't pay. What he could do was tell stories. That was his line of work.

He told you a story about a mask. A Colombian funerary mask, that's what Dickie called it. Solid gold. It had a lot of history, this mask. It had been through the hands of the royal families of Europe and caused at least one revolution. For hundreds of years, people had been stealing and killing for it. Gold, and beautiful. Nothing else like it anywhere in the world. And behind it a trail of bodies, centuries long.

Campbell told you about this mask, told you he had a line on it, he got you interested. He told you about it so you wouldn't kill him, but he must have told too much. He didn't keep himself vital. You thought you didn't need him, so he got a twist in his neck, one more hole in the side of his head.

> *Swagger lay outside Holcomb's. He waited half in,*
> *half out the phone booth. He meant to shoot*
> *_____ and me, he meant to hang the corpse on us.*
> *But as Swagger's voice fills everything*
> *I can feel my hands round Holcomb's neck,*
> *I can see _____ bouncing him off the walls,*
> *and Cansel putting the final hole in his cheek.*

Soon Lowden the amateur in antiques, and in crime,

was overtaken by the curse, his overstuffed body left to dream of an inheritance it would never get. And then the trail of death caught up to your little gang, didn't it? Even the ghoul, Cansel, couldn't escape. By the time I got to him your little friend had already shot and stabbed him, and set fire to the hotel room he was lying in. He was a ghoul from hell right up to the end: he died in flames, burned up, until the skin slid from his bones.

That was to be my pleasure, killing Cansel, but your friend took it from me.

Which left Dickie, a last loose end. Childs and I were there, in Dickie's dingy little office home, when your friend shot him. The shot came from the dark of the fire escape, and Dickie was down, the red muck and broken china of his head spread across thin carpet. We shot back, and when your friend ran for it, we went after him, Childs down the front steps, me down the fire escape. In the street I almost ran through Cromarty as he climbed from a prowl car. For a moment I thought I would have to take a swing at him to stay on my man, but he shouted, 'Well? Come on!' and we chased after our man together. In the middle of a crossing he stopped, Box. He raised his head like he was sniffing at the air. And I took my shot.

> There's so much Swagger, he is everywhere and
> there's no me, not a dot, not a drop of sweat.
> I ask, What happened to the mask?
> The package, like a baby wrapped up so tight it might
> have just come in the mail. Who got the mask?

I'll tell you, Box.

A gold Colombian death mask, and plenty are dead for it now. Only there's no mask. Campbell made it up. He realised he needed to give you something to save his life and he had nothing to give, so he told a story. He made it good enough to stick, too. Cansel bought it, and everywhere he went looking for the mask he convinced someone else, until Lowden bought it, and Dickie. Your friend bought it. All for a story, he said. All for nothing.

————

Polly realises she's holding a half-eaten apple. She can't remember taking a bite. She thinks about when she found out she was pregnant with the child who would be Evvie. The shock of it: for her and for Chester. 'Our concern, Box,' she says, 'was that we'd both raised some heck in our time, and we thought we might end up raising another little piece of it in the form of this child.'

Everything was more complicated than that, of course. Evvie was an angel for a normal duration of blessedness, and then a squalling demon for a period almost too short to be remembered once it was past, which at the time felt longer than a prison sentence, and louder, with fewer moments of rest. Then, gradually, over not so many years, what appeared in her was the intelligent, headstrong, caring person she would be for the rest of her days.

*

Polly's favourite moments in life, particularly after Chester's death, came during those evenings—they came once or twice a year—when Evvie would sit and talk with her in intense, one-sided conversations on large questions: on living and how it should be done, or the obstacles she'd found to being principled or kind or forgiving. These talks felt like examinations that Evvie gave to herself on the condition of her soul, and it was clear Polly contributed best by being silent.

'I learned to keep my counsel,' Polly says. 'You know how it is.'

One day, Evvie read half a dozen lines in the newspaper—about a girl who had walked into the hospital after a mangled abortion and died three days later. 'This little girl walked in there holding her blood and pieces of her own uterus in her hands, that was how wrong the operation had gone. It made Evvie so angry,' says Polly. 'Who wouldn't be angry? There were decisions that led to that young girl in that state, and they weren't the girl's decisions. They were the decisions of men who thought it was better to send her to a butcher than give her medical care and some control over herself. I would have read that in the newspaper and been angry for days and done nothing.'

Evvie read it and started planning. She had Dr Boken, and Dr Boken would have done anything for her. She had drugs, and books, and clean equipment, and she meant to make things better for any girls in that same sorry situation.

'And it was no use telling her that the same men who made the laws which killed that girl would work to find her and punish her for it,' says Polly.

'Of course,' she says, 'you found her instead, didn't you, Box?'

Polly is writing a letter, she has it on top of a book on her lap, leans on the book to write it. It takes time. When she finishes, she folds it and puts it into an envelope, puts the envelope into her bag. It's early still but she doesn't want to be in this room any more. She's been here long enough.

She pulls her chair around, between Box and the window, so that as she sits her knees touch his right leg. He is big but he doesn't look strong any more: he looks punctured, drained, spent. He looks like he is weeks dead and lying in the undergrowth of that hair and beard, the frame of that device just so much broken fencing. She waves a hand in front of his eyes and says, 'Box.' She taps at the device with a finger as if she is knocking on a door.

Does he see her? Does she swim up to the windshield of whatever there is left of him? If she does there's no sign of it.

'Well, Box,' she says. 'I've sat here thinking with you and it's taken me a long time, but not all my time. I'm not going to let this be the rest of my life. I've done my thinking,' she says. 'And I still aim to forgive you some day, Box, because this hate I have for you is no good to sit in. But I don't need to be here to do it, and you don't need to be there.'

She stands, folds her chair and puts it against the wall, and leaves him.

———

Somehow I press my way out of Swagger, I fight my way clear and run from Holcomb's building, and look back and it has the great and golden face of the detective, and I run and climb into cracks through drifting, leaking, poisoned thought, and go back to Evvie. The device can fix everything if it can just fix this.

I crawl back up this branch I'm on where I wasn't good enough for her and she didn't care to be with me. But I rush. And I make a mistake. I make worse than mistakes.

I lower the device around my head and fit the straps. I am one of Holcomb's scientists climbing into his machine. I leak thought and begin to flicker, a card in a shuffling deck. I go to Evvie and go to her and go to her. Not because I'm going to exhaust her, but because in some part of some inclination in her exists a desire to care for me and be with me. As real as anything I have ever felt it's there and it only needs to be found, that amenable fraction of a possibility. If I can't find it alone I send emissaries, I split the work, I play the odds.

We each of us crawl back through time and go to her and the same thing every time—she says these kindnesses

were a mistake and not to be repeated, and we keep crawling back but we can't find a way to hold her, to keep her
caring for us.

We get impatient. We parade in front of her together,
and it scares her, but each of us is so keen to be cared for,
to make it all work. We tell her that we know that there is
some part of her that loves us, some part that can entertain
being with us, so what are our odds? 1 in 1000? A thousand of us stand in front of her, which of the thousand is
it, we just need you to find the right one and he'll care for
you as you care for him. Except she is scared—there's so
many of us.

In the great part of me, what I want for her is only comfort and care, and her happiness before anything else. I am
good and selfless in my love for her. But there is, in some
small part, something less good. So in all the thousands of
us, there are those that are angry, who can even hate her,
who think that if she can seem to despise us now then she
was false and cheap when she seemed to love us, when she
kissed us or took our hand. Fights break out between us,
and the worst are subdued or killed, but there's always
more—vicious, selfish.

We rush and everything is confused and a lot is bloody,
and still we don't know how to hold it all and keep it.
Some of us lose our minds—we'll make her understand,
we'll make her.

Some of us despair. A sour mood can sweep through

us: the most soured give in to it, they put their necks into ropes and step onto tracks, and their bodies pile up like sandbags. Terrible impulses turn to pitched battles, the piles grow bigger.

Some of all these probabilities tear each other apart and the number of us reduces, there are fewer and fewer. We crawl up the branch, we keep at it, but slowly, with care, there's not so many of us, already we have some sense, seen that things should not be rushed, not in the way they have been.

Only there are still some terrible impulses. One of them goes to see Evvie alone.

There is a phone call and it wakes me, and at first I take the confusion to be mine.

But even this can be fixed and undone. Work carefully and slowly. If I sit and think then that is enough, that is plenty. One of them can scrabble up the branch as many times as it takes, to make it all right and fix these mistakes, can find the single thread that has to be pulled to noose all this disaster and blood. Evvie alive again, and _____, and Holcomb too. However long it takes.

However long it takes, it will have been cheaply earned.

Epilogue

Hector and Charles wake early. At breakfast, Hector rereads his letter. 'Read it aloud if you are going to read it,' says Charles.

'You know what it says,' says Hector.

'As do you,' says Charles, 'but you are electing to read it instead of engaging in conversation, in which case you can read it aloud.'

Hector looks at Charles wearily, but returns to the first page of the letter, gives a small cough intended to be obnoxious, and reads.

To Hector,

I don't suppose you would know me, but years ago you knew my husband and maybe this address for you is still good. My husband had some unsavoury friends once, and I hope you don't mind me saying I count you among them. I am now too old a lady for that to mean much, and also people indulge ladies of my age when they come out with rudeness and I hope you will too.

The first thing I should tell you is that Chester, my husband, has died. I am sorry not to have written to you with regards to the funeral but there was a long time where my husband felt sure he was dying, long enough that we spoke about his wishes for when he was gone, and he wished principally to keep the funeral small and cheap. I am sure you don't care about this and I realise I am trying to be polite because I am writing to a stranger with a request and I should make myself get to the reason of this letter, which is that I am hoping that you will be able to kill the man who is responsible for the death of my daughter.

I know you will see that I am inexperienced at this, so I can only reassure you that I am serious about it, I have done a lot of thinking before taking these steps, and I include some money to show it, though there is as much available to you as you will tell me is fair for the job.

I hope that the police don't read this letter somehow and arrest me for it and whatever you do, whether you can help me and my husband or not, I hope you will keep my confidence.

The man I would like you to kill is called Box, he lives now in one of two madhouses we have in our city. I will put a phone number where I can be reached at the end of this letter and I will give you more information but he will not be hard to find, as in more than a year I have not seen him move even to scratch himself. He is a very big man but quite mad, and will not be difficult to kill.

Please do understand that this letter is not a joke.

Polly Heydt

Hector hands the letter to Charles, who is dabbing some grains of salt that are scattered on the table and touching them to his tongue. He looks over it and says, 'A letter with some promise. From a nice lady, it would seem.'

Hector nods. 'We should go and do as she asks,' he says.

They make their way to Box by colour, following the corridor until it turns red and then turning to their left and there is the door. Even the position of his seat has been given to them, and when they reach the room it is just as described. He sits by the window, the device balanced on his head, like a nest made from refuse, or a trap he has become caught in.

The instant Charles puts a foot into the room, Box begins to turn. The movement is slow, monumental, like a planet steered on ropes. Box's head turns to them, the dull cabinets of his eyes lighting up.

Hector laughs. 'My God,' he says and laughs again. He looks from Charles to Box and Box to Charles. 'What a wonderful thing. You're the double of him. The absolute double. Or you would be if you had fallen into a creek for a hundred years.'

Charles snorts in amusement. He looks at the face under the wild hair and the trellis around it, and scratches at the stubble of his own cheek. 'There is a likeness, it's true,' he says.

'A likeness!' laughs Hector. 'You are the image of each other.'

His eyes fixed on Box, Charles touches the side of his own head, as if expecting to find the weight of the device there.

'It's like witnessing a haunting,' says Hector. 'As if you have grave-robbed your own corpse.'

Meanwhile Box is looking at Charles as he hasn't looked at anything for years. Water tips from his eyes. His mouth shudders. On unsure legs, he stands.

Hector places himself by the wall, sidesteps there, watching too eagerly to turn away. Box, with wet eyes shaking with life, stumbles to Charles, one arm out, and Charles catches him and holds him upright. They lean into each other as two sides of an arch, Box shaking, Charles fighting each shake, using all his strength to keep the other man standing.

Finally Box is stable and can stand on his own. The forward edge of the device almost touches the other man's forehead. Box waits, eyes wide and fearful, for the man to say something to him, torment pulls at Box's eyes, and he wipes at them.

He speaks. 'Wh at is it?' he asks Charles. 'We m ade it good, m ade it right? We fo und the w ay?' The spasms of his vocal cords mean he has to draw the words from his throat, each one takes time to fill with breathy sound.

Charles grins at Hector, who simply shrugs in response. Charles lifts his hands and reaches for the rear strap, one of the two that fixes the device in place. He moves slowly, steadily, and when his hands touch Box's ear, his fingers moving to the buckle, Box flinches inward, his eyes close, but he says nothing. Charles lifts the end of the strap and, with some difficulty, undoes it. One hand stays, gripping the device, balancing it, while the other reaches for the other buckle at Box's chin. As Charles undoes it, his hand grows wet with Box's tears. Box's eyes stay tightly shut and Charles lifts the device. He passes it to Hector who steps forward to receive it.

Through Box's beard and hair are rubbed friction lines where nothing grows and the flesh is purple or else white and pulls from itself in scabs that look like fingernails or scales. There are sores at the edges of his hairline, at the right corner of his jaw, to the side of his left eye, his lips are cracked and bleeding and his crying eyes rest in his face at the bottom of deep red seams. With the device gone he is only more bent than before, as if a weight has been added to him rather than taken away. He opens his eyes which still pour water—he is an overrunning sink. 'P lease,' he says. 'W hat is it? We m ade it ri ght?'

Charles, amused, looks at Hector, who takes the letter from his jacket pocket and hands it to Charles, who holds it out to Box. 'Can you read?' he asks. 'Read this.' Box can't work his hands, they curl in on themselves, they are hands made hooves, but he manages to take the letter. He attempts to read, but understands almost none of it. He signals his incomprehension in gulps.

Charles, as if moved to pity, steps into Box and embraces him.

Box feels the embrace as absolution come at last.

His image takes hold of him warmly, strongly, and he feels time pressing against itself, two fundamental forces clasping each other, pressed together in kindness, until he could belong equally to either of the two bodies, and the specifics of the one—the pain in the back, the itchiness of the sores that ring his head, all his other pains and, beneath them all, his remorse and the mess he carries—all quickly halve, and then, having lost their centre, disperse, upwards, into lightness.

Charles, his right arm around Box's back, puts with his right hand the knife into Box's quivering throat, holds, as if for applause, and then lets him drop.

The End

Goodbye